VALERIAN AND LAURELINE

THE ORDER OF THE STONES

J.-C. MÉZIÈRES AND **P. CHRISTIN**
COLOURS: E. TRANLI

CINEBOOK
The 9th Art Publisher

VALERIAN was born in Galaxity, megapolis of future Earth. In 2713 he joined the Spatio-temporal Service. Virtuoso spaceship pilot and disciplined agent, he began to criss-cross time and space to confront any danger that could threaten his planet – now one of the galaxy's greatest powers.

Laureline, on the other hand, hails from the Middle Ages, where she lived in untamed forests and occasionally moonlighted as a unicorn. She saved Valerian's life during a mission to those troubled times where sorcery and technology could come together to modify Earth's past … and therefore its future.

The two young agents' combined talents could not prevent a nuclear explosion from causing New York City to be swallowed by the sea in 1986. But a few years later they changed the future instead in order to cancel the cataclysm. Unfortunately, that extremely risky operation caused the Earth of the future to disappear from the known universe!

No longer receiving orders, their embassy gone from Point Central – the gigantic artificial world where every species and civilisation of the galaxy meet in a sort of multicoloured UN – all Valerian and Laureline have left to survive is their spaceship. They take on missions that lead them to the most bizarre worlds.

They have allies in their tasks: the exasperating Shingouz spies, the terrible Schniarfer or the wonderful Mr Albert, their contact in nowadays Paris. Enemies, too, such as the false gods of Hypsis, Sat the Fallen Archangel or the Triumvirate that rules over planet Rubanis. Not to mention massive, forbidding black stones no one's ever heard about.

Valerian is a comic series without parallel, in that there isn't really a present in its narration; no possible beginning or end as long as the universe exists. Which doesn't mean there is no suspense! Will Valerian and Laureline ever find the vanished Earth again?

That is the subject of a new cycle of adventures that will take them from the mysteries of the Great Void to the revelations of the Time Opener.

Original title: Valerian – L'Ordre des Pierres
Original edition: © Dargaud Paris, 2007 by Christin, Mezières & Tranlé
www.dargaud.com
All rights reserved
English translation: © 2016 Cinebook Ltd
Translator: Jerome Saincantin
Editor: Lisa Morris
Lettering and text layout: Design Amorandi
Printed in Spain by EGEDSA
This edition first published in Great Britain in 2017 by
Cinebook Ltd
56 Beech Avenue
Canterbury, Kent
CT4 7TA
www.cinebook.com
A CIP catalogue record for this book
is available from the British Library
ISBN 978-1-84918-336-9

9th CINEBOOK
The 9th Art Publisher

IN THE **GREAT VOID**, WHERE THERE ARE NO MORE STARS, NO KNOWN SPACE ROUTES, WHERE THE UNIVERSE IN FORMATION KEEPS EXPANDING, FULL (OR EMPTY – NO ONE KNOWS) OF MYSTERIES, DANGERS, PERHAPS EVEN RICHES... A SKIFF LEAVES THE CAVERNOUS INNARDS OF THE GIGANTIC EXPLORATION SHIP BELONGING TO CAPTAIN SINGH'A ROOG'A AND HER MOTLEY CREW.

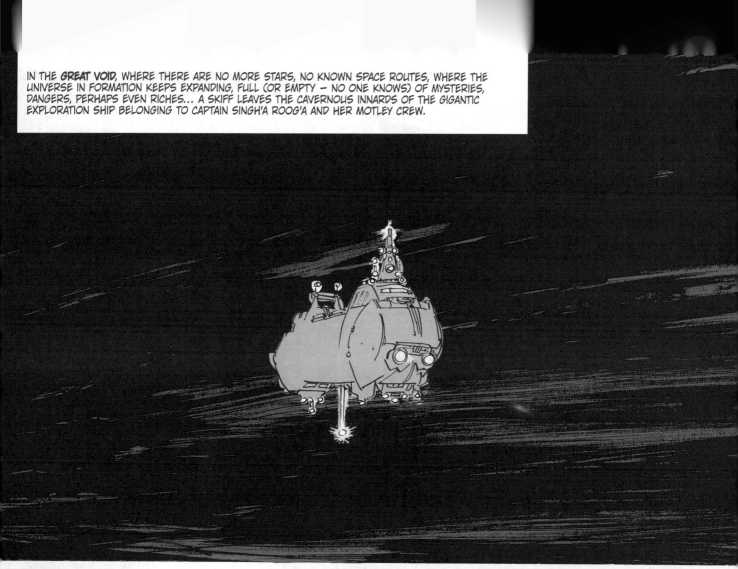

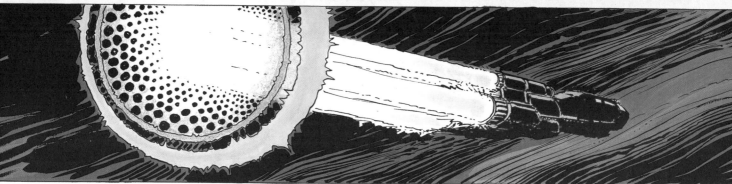

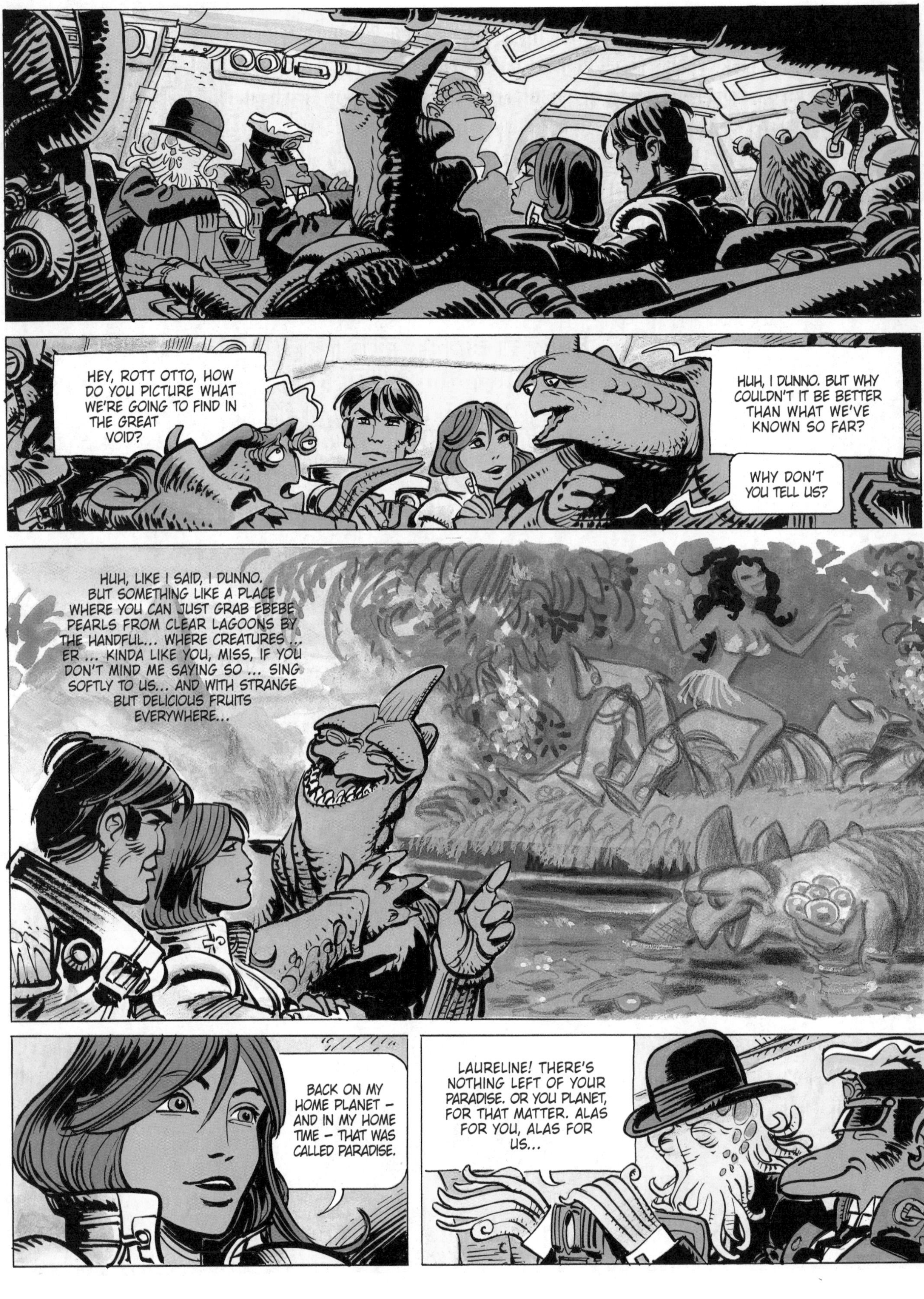
HEY, ROTT OTTO, HOW DO YOU PICTURE WHAT WE'RE GOING TO FIND IN THE GREAT VOID?
HUH, I DUNNO. BUT WHY COULDN'T IT BE BETTER THAN WHAT WE'VE KNOWN SO FAR?
WHY DON'T YOU TELL US?
HUH, LIKE I SAID, I DUNNO. BUT SOMETHING LIKE A PLACE WHERE YOU CAN JUST GRAB EBEBE PEARLS FROM CLEAR LAGOONS BY THE HANDFUL... WHERE CREATURES ... ER ... KINDA LIKE YOU, MISS, IF YOU DON'T MIND ME SAYING SO ... SING SOFTLY TO US... AND WITH STRANGE BUT DELICIOUS FRUITS EVERYWHERE...
BACK ON MY HOME PLANET – AND IN MY HOME TIME – THAT WAS CALLED PARADISE.
LAURELINE! THERE'S NOTHING LEFT OF YOUR PARADISE. OR YOU PLANET, FOR THAT MATTER. ALAS FOR YOU, ALAS FOR US...
2

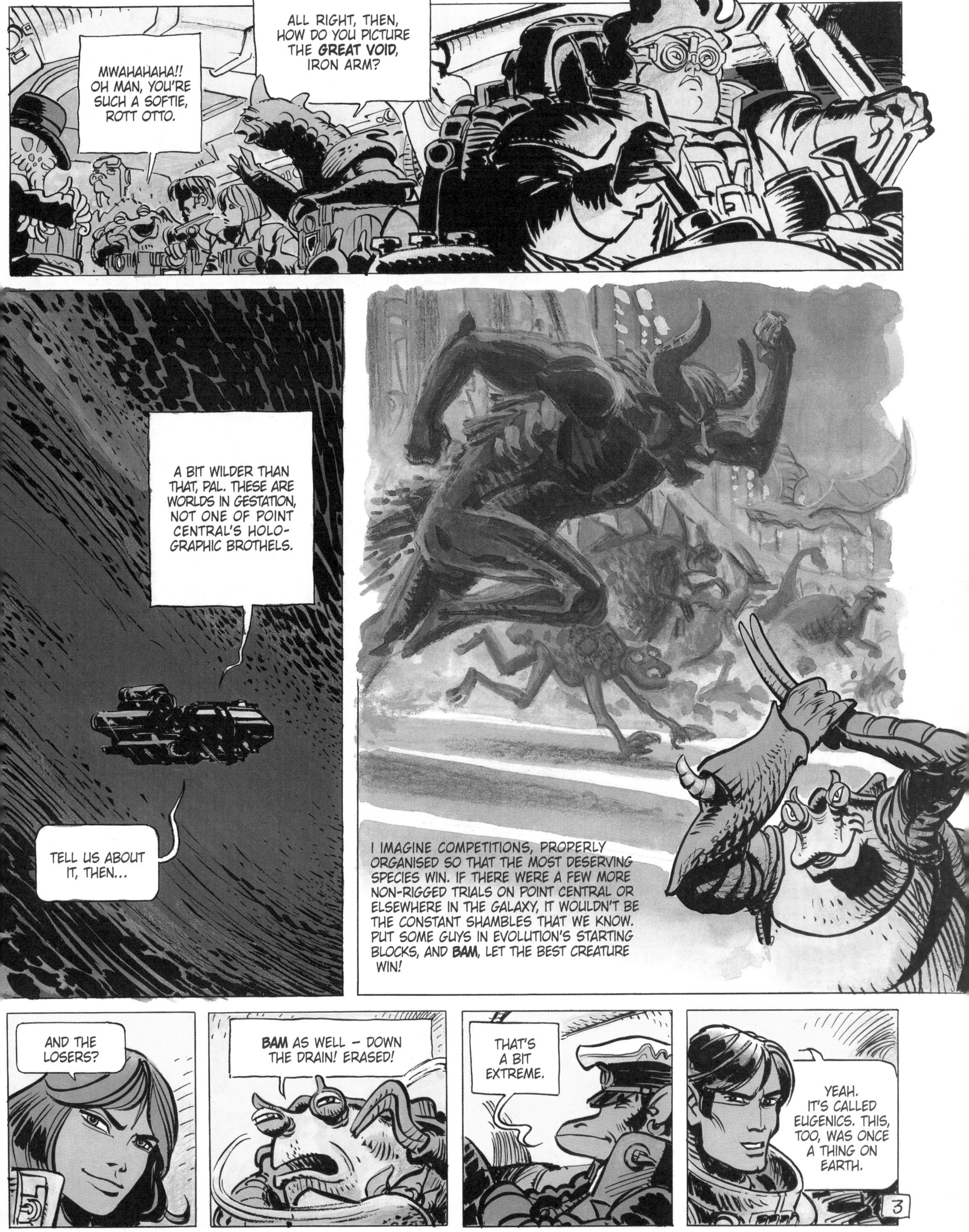
MWAHAHAHA!! OH MAN, YOU'RE SUCH A SOFTIE, ROTT OTTO.
ALL RIGHT, THEN, HOW DO YOU PICTURE THE **GREAT VOID**, IRON ARM?
A BIT WILDER THAN THAT, PAL. THESE ARE WORLDS IN GESTATION, NOT ONE OF POINT CENTRAL'S HOLO-GRAPHIC BROTHELS.
TELL US ABOUT IT, THEN...
I IMAGINE COMPETITIONS, PROPERLY ORGANISED SO THAT THE MOST DESERVING SPECIES WIN. IF THERE WERE A FEW MORE NON-RIGGED TRIALS ON POINT CENTRAL OR ELSEWHERE IN THE GALAXY, IT WOULDN'T BE THE CONSTANT SHAMBLES THAT WE KNOW. PUT SOME GUYS IN EVOLUTION'S STARTING BLOCKS, AND **BAM**, LET THE BEST CREATURE WIN!
AND THE LOSERS?
BAM AS WELL – DOWN THE DRAIN! ERASED!
THAT'S A BIT EXTREME.
YEAH. IT'S CALLED EUGENICS. THIS, TOO, WAS ONCE A THING ON EARTH.
3

HOW DO YOU IMAGINE IT, LOOTENANT?

ME?

I'D LIKE TO BELIEVE IN A PLACE BORN PERFECT OUT OF CHAOS. ROCK WOULD SPONTANEOUSLY FORM INTO HARMONIOUS ARCHITECTURE; EVER-CLEAR WATER WOULD FLOW THROUGH NATURAL CANALS BRIDGED BY ELEGANTLY PLACED ARCHES; THE INHABITANTS WOULD BE MONOSEXUAL, TO PREVENT ANY CONFLICTS...

LIEUTENANT MOLTO CORTES, YOUR AESTHETICISM IS GETTING THE BETTER OF YOU. THERE HAS NEVER BEEN, NOR WILL THERE EVER BE, SUCH A PLACE IN THE UNIVERSE. NO MORE IN THE CURRENT ONE THAN IN THE ONE TO COME.

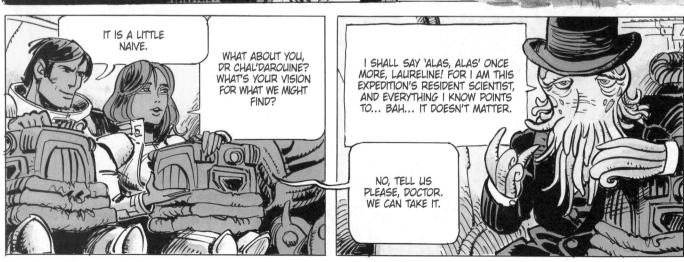

IT IS A LITTLE NAIVE.

WHAT ABOUT YOU, DR CHAL'DAROUINE? WHAT'S YOUR VISION FOR WHAT WE MIGHT FIND?

I SHALL SAY 'ALAS, ALAS' ONCE MORE, LAURELINE! FOR I AM THIS EXPEDITION'S RESIDENT SCIENTIST, AND EVERYTHING I KNOW POINTS TO... BAH... IT DOESN'T MATTER.

NO, TELL US PLEASE, DOCTOR. WE CAN TAKE IT.

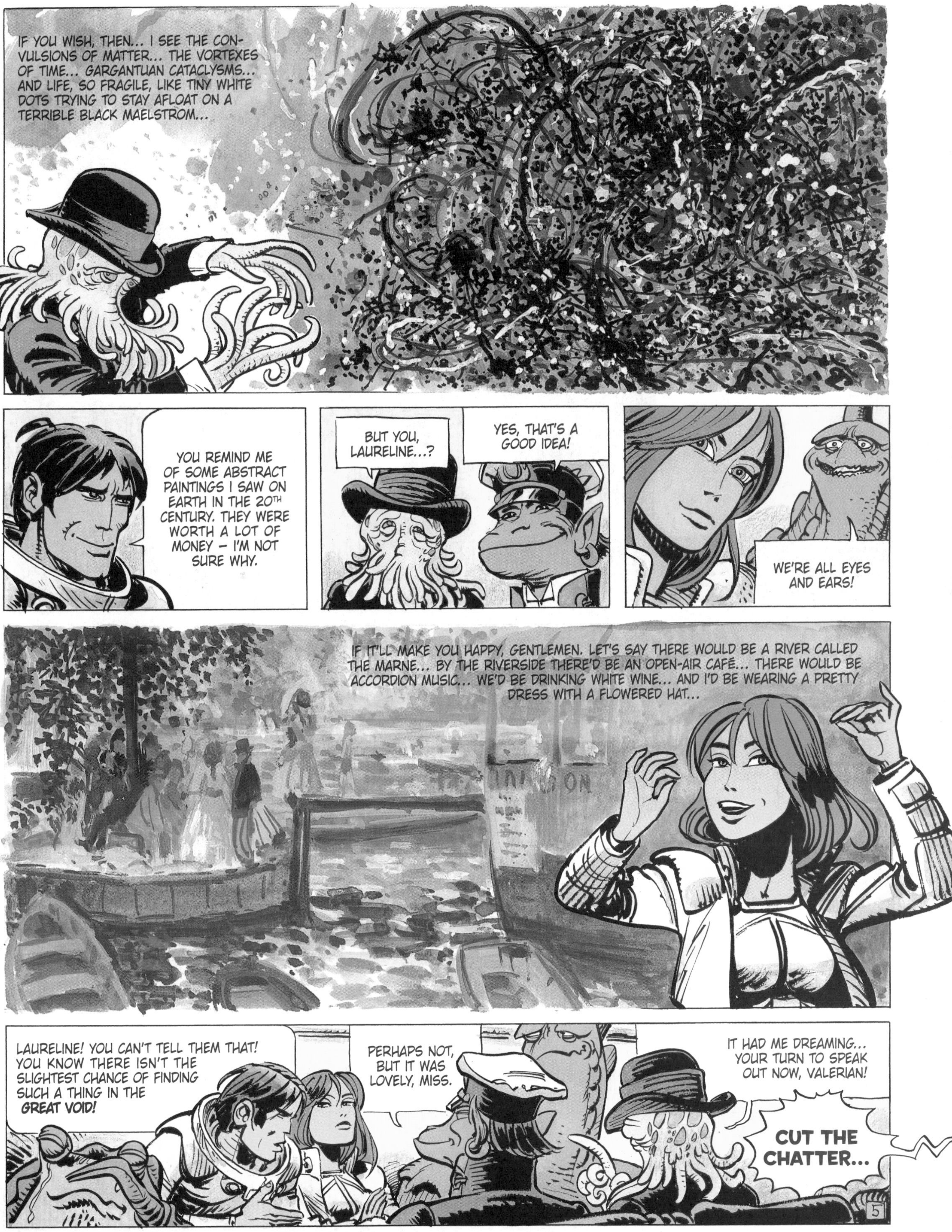
IF YOU WISH, THEN... I SEE THE CONVULSIONS OF MATTER... THE VORTEXES OF TIME... GARGANTUAN CATACLYSMS... AND LIFE, SO FRAGILE, LIKE TINY WHITE DOTS TRYING TO STAY AFLOAT ON A TERRIBLE BLACK MAELSTROM...
YOU REMIND ME OF SOME ABSTRACT PAINTINGS I SAW ON EARTH IN THE 20TH CENTURY. THEY WERE WORTH A LOT OF MONEY – I'M NOT SURE WHY.
BUT YOU, LAURELINE...?
YES, THAT'S A GOOD IDEA!
WE'RE ALL EYES AND EARS!
IF IT'LL MAKE YOU HAPPY, GENTLEMEN. LET'S SAY THERE WOULD BE A RIVER CALLED THE MARNE... BY THE RIVERSIDE THERE'D BE AN OPEN-AIR CAFÉ... THERE WOULD BE ACCORDION MUSIC... WE'D BE DRINKING WHITE WINE... AND I'D BE WEARING A PRETTY DRESS WITH A FLOWERED HAT...
LAURELINE! YOU CAN'T TELL THEM THAT! YOU KNOW THERE ISN'T THE SLIGHTEST CHANCE OF FINDING SUCH A THING IN THE **GREAT VOID!**
PERHAPS NOT, BUT IT WAS LOVELY, MISS.
IT HAD ME DREAMING... YOUR TURN TO SPEAK OUT NOW, VALERIAN!
CUT THE CHATTER...
5

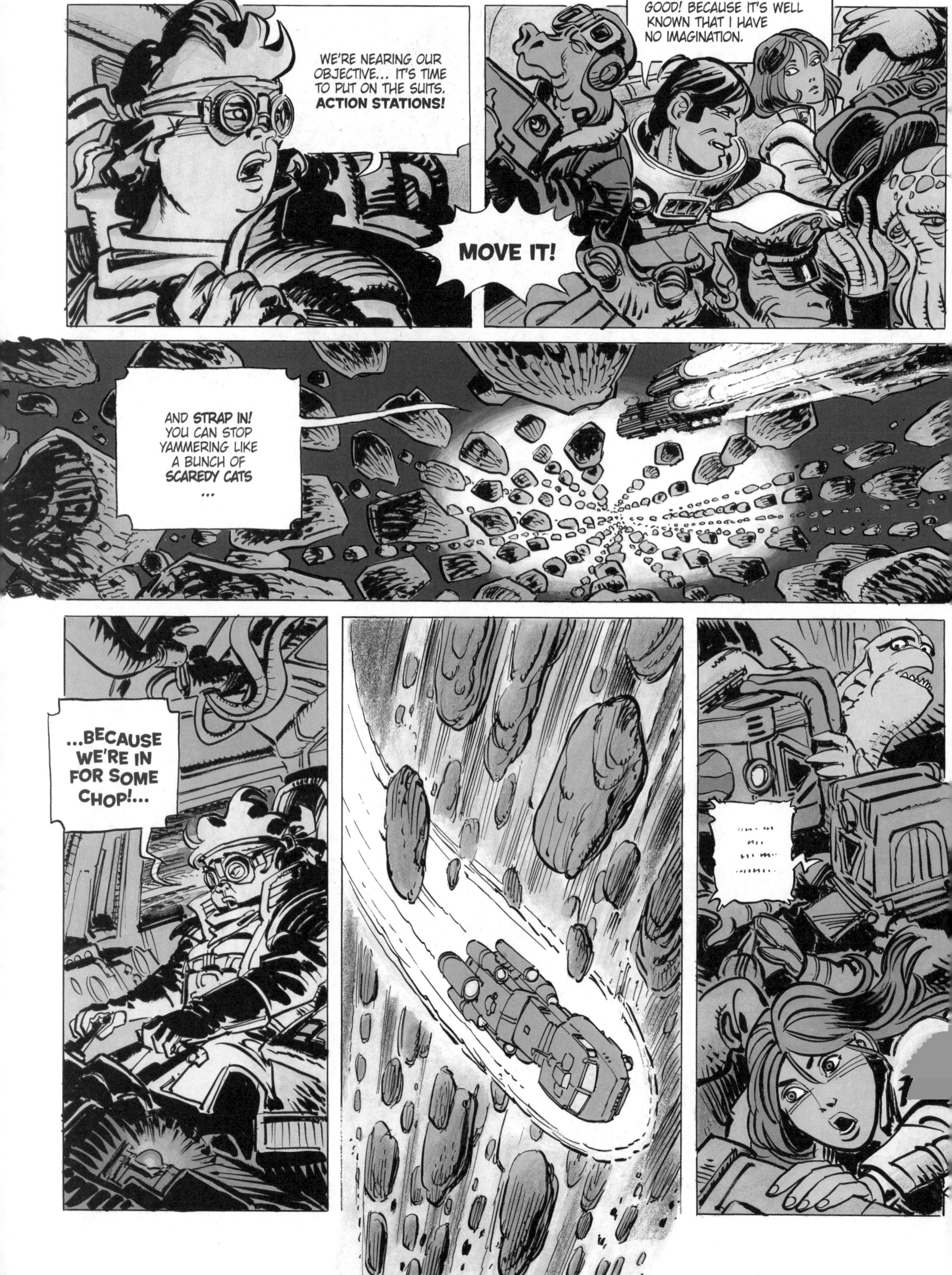
WE'RE NEARING OUR OBJECTIVE... IT'S TIME TO PUT ON THE SUITS. ACTION STATIONS!
GOOD! BECAUSE IT'S WELL KNOWN THAT I HAVE NO IMAGINATION.
MOVE IT!
AND STRAP IN! YOU CAN STOP YAMMERING LIKE A BUNCH OF SCAREDY CATS ...
...BECAUSE WE'RE IN FOR SOME CHOP!...

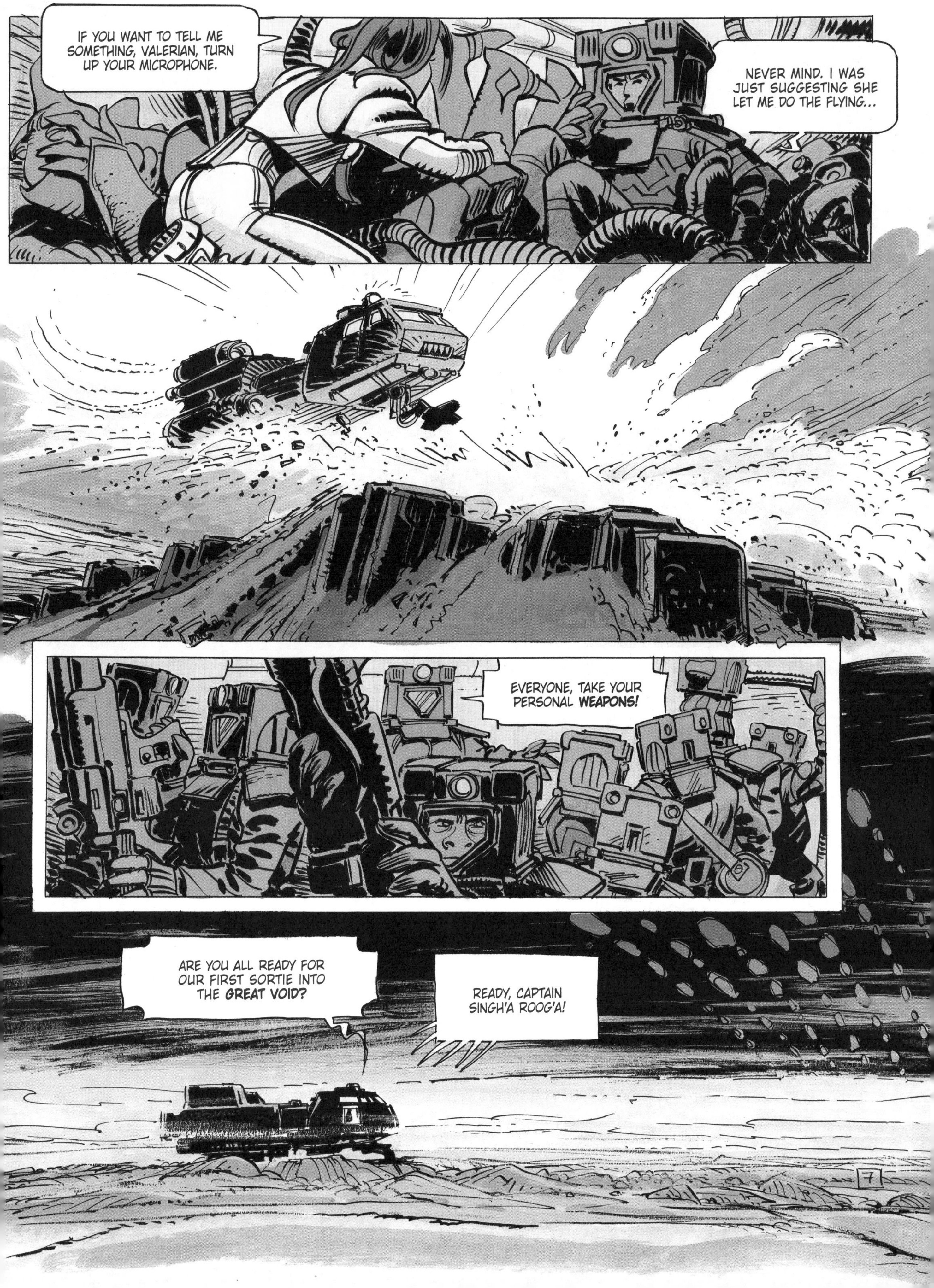
IF YOU WANT TO TELL ME SOMETHING, VALERIAN, TURN UP YOUR MICROPHONE.
NEVER MIND. I WAS JUST SUGGESTING SHE LET ME DO THE FLYING...
EVERYONE, TAKE YOUR PERSONAL **WEAPONS!**
ARE YOU ALL READY FOR OUR FIRST SORTIE INTO THE **GREAT VOID?**
READY, CAPTAIN SINGH'A ROOG'A!
7

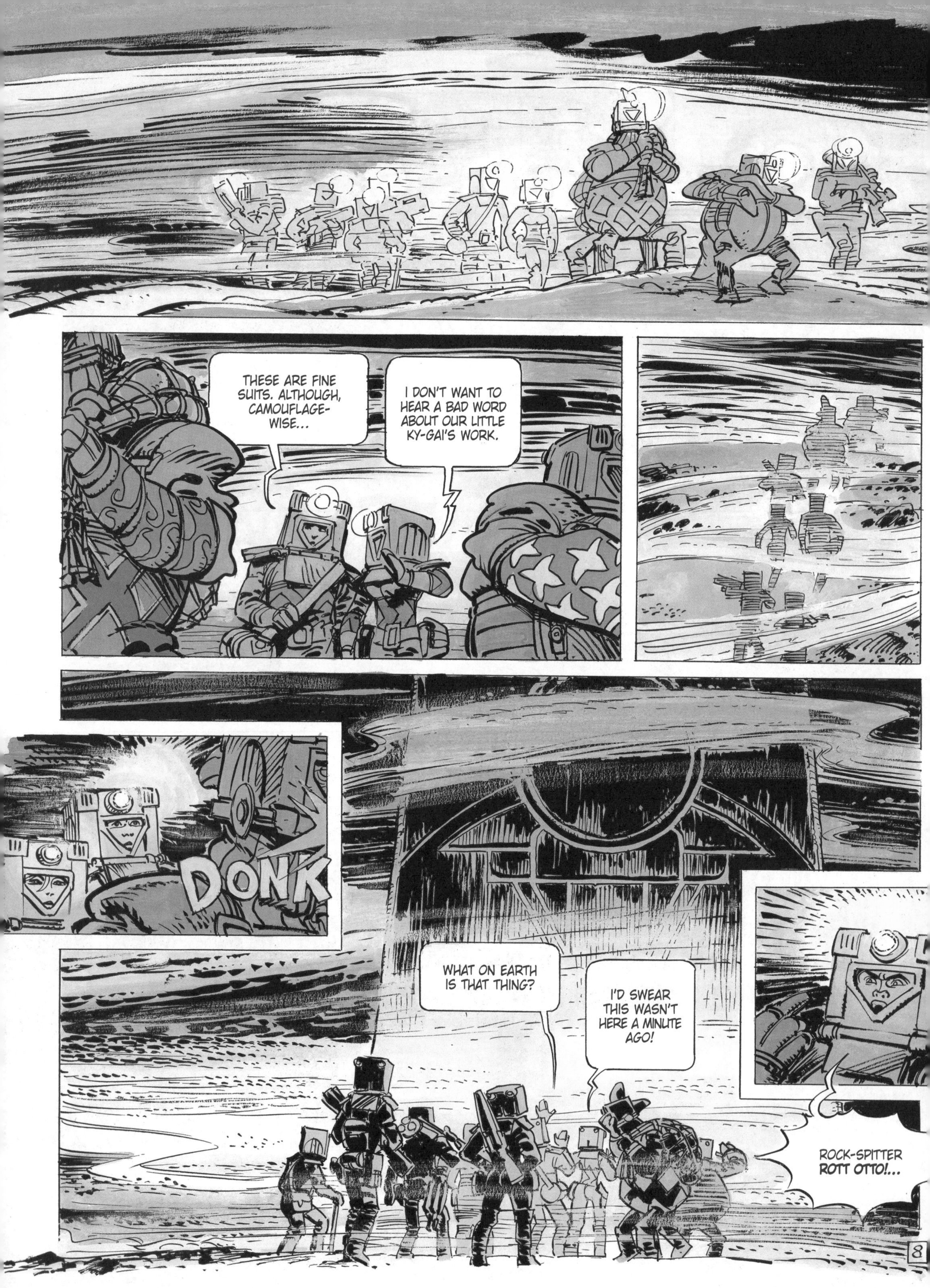
THESE ARE FINE SUITS. ALTHOUGH, CAMOUFLAGE-WISE...
I DON'T WANT TO HEAR A BAD WORD ABOUT OUR LITTLE KY-GAI'S WORK.
DONK
WHAT ON EARTH IS THAT THING?
I'D SWEAR THIS WASN'T HERE A MINUTE AGO!
ROCK-SPITTER ROTT OTTO!...
8

GET THIS OUT OF MY WAY!

AYE AYE, CAPTAIN!

JUST NEED TO EAT A LITTLE AMMO, AND...

B-ROOO

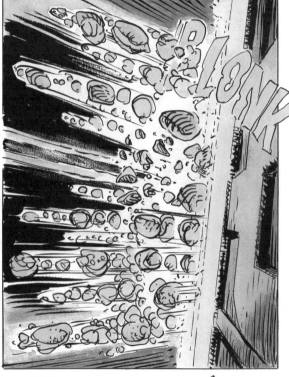

BLONK

SO MUCH FOR THAT. YOUR TURN...

MOLTO CORTES!

GZEEE

IRON ARM!

SCHLAPF

CAPTAIN?

FAILED AGAIN! SO IT'S MY TURN!

VLOOF

I THINK WE'RE WASTING OUR TIME, CAPTAIN. TAKE A LOOK BEHIND US.

MORE OF THOSE ... ER ... THINGS!

WHERE DID OUR SKIFF GO?

THEY WEREN'T THERE A MINUTE AGO EITHER!

LOOK! THEY'RE FLOATING ABOVE THE GROUND!

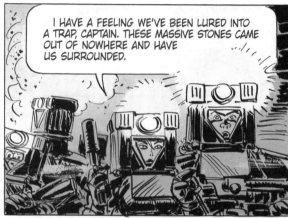

I HAVE A FEELING WE'VE BEEN LURED INTO A TRAP, CAPTAIN. THESE MASSIVE STONES CAME OUT OF NOWHERE AND HAVE US SURROUNDED.

WE NEED TO GET A CLEARER IDEA...

COMING, VALERIAN.

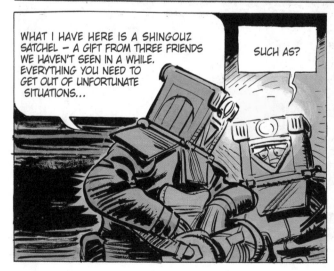

WHAT I HAVE HERE IS A SHINGOUZ SATCHEL — A GIFT FROM THREE FRIENDS WE HAVEN'T SEEN IN A WHILE. EVERYTHING YOU NEED TO GET OUT OF UNFORTUNATE SITUATIONS...

SUCH AS?

A WALL-PIERCING WAVES EAR TRUMPET...

A SEE-THROUGH SCOPE... AND A FEW OTHER GADGETS, ALL SYRTIAN-MADE.

12

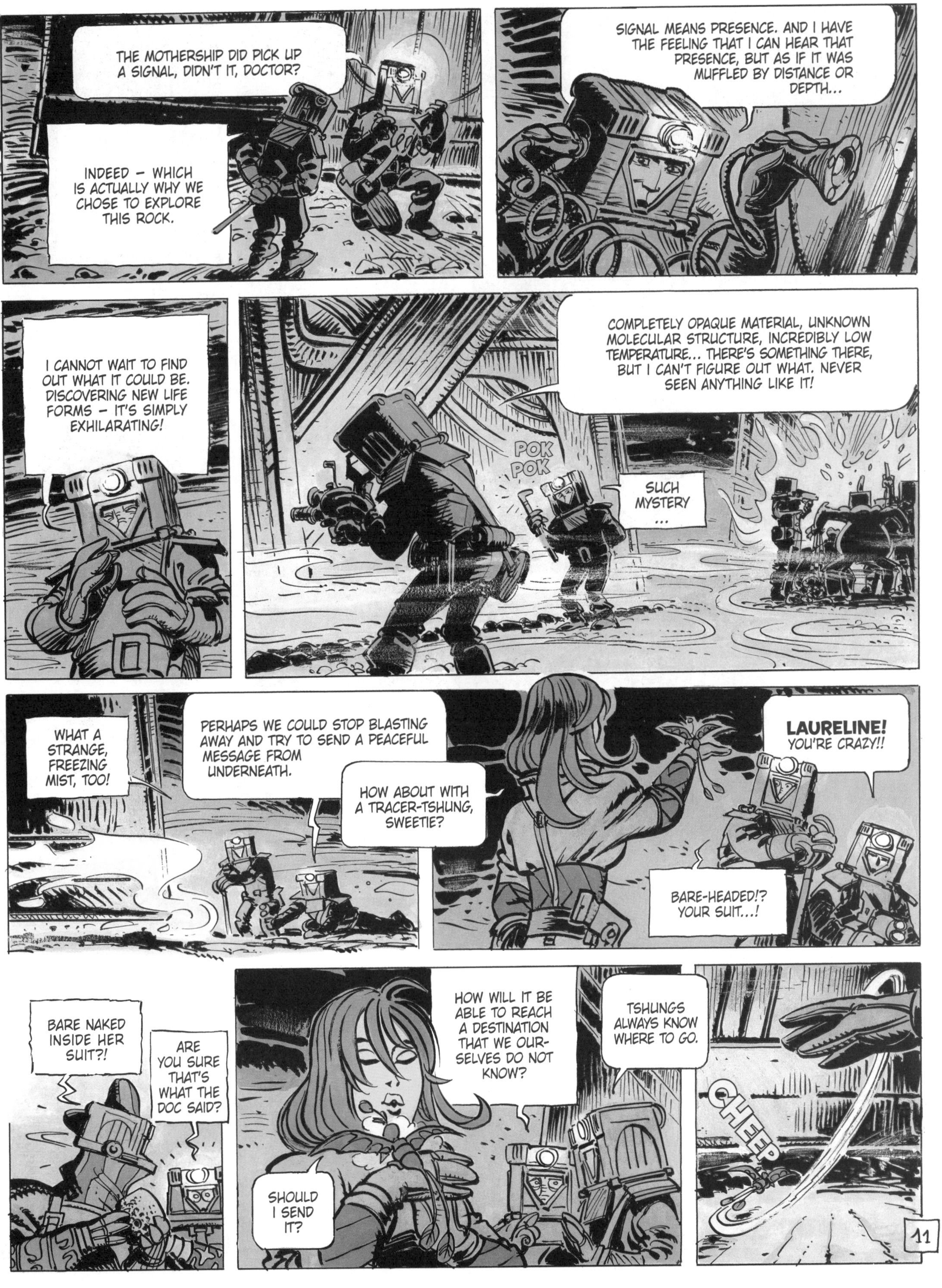
THE MOTHERSHIP DID PICK UP A SIGNAL, DIDN'T IT, DOCTOR?
INDEED – WHICH IS ACTUALLY WHY WE CHOSE TO EXPLORE THIS ROCK.
SIGNAL MEANS PRESENCE. AND I HAVE THE FEELING THAT I CAN HEAR THAT PRESENCE, BUT AS IF IT WAS MUFFLED BY DISTANCE OR DEPTH...
I CANNOT WAIT TO FIND OUT WHAT IT COULD BE. DISCOVERING NEW LIFE FORMS – IT'S SIMPLY EXHILARATING!
COMPLETELY OPAQUE MATERIAL, UNKNOWN MOLECULAR STRUCTURE, INCREDIBLY LOW TEMPERATURE... THERE'S SOMETHING THERE, BUT I CAN'T FIGURE OUT WHAT. NEVER SEEN ANYTHING LIKE IT!
POK POK
SUCH MYSTERY ...
WHAT A STRANGE, FREEZING MIST, TOO!
PERHAPS WE COULD STOP BLASTING AWAY AND TRY TO SEND A PEACEFUL MESSAGE FROM UNDERNEATH.
HOW ABOUT WITH A TRACER-TSHUNG, SWEETIE?
LAURELINE! YOU'RE CRAZY!!
BARE-HEADED!? YOUR SUIT...!
BARE NAKED INSIDE HER SUIT?!
ARE YOU SURE THAT'S WHAT THE DOC SAID?
HOW WILL IT BE ABLE TO REACH A DESTINATION THAT WE OUR-SELVES DO NOT KNOW?
SHOULD I SEND IT?
TSHUNGS ALWAYS KNOW WHERE TO GO.
CHEEP
11

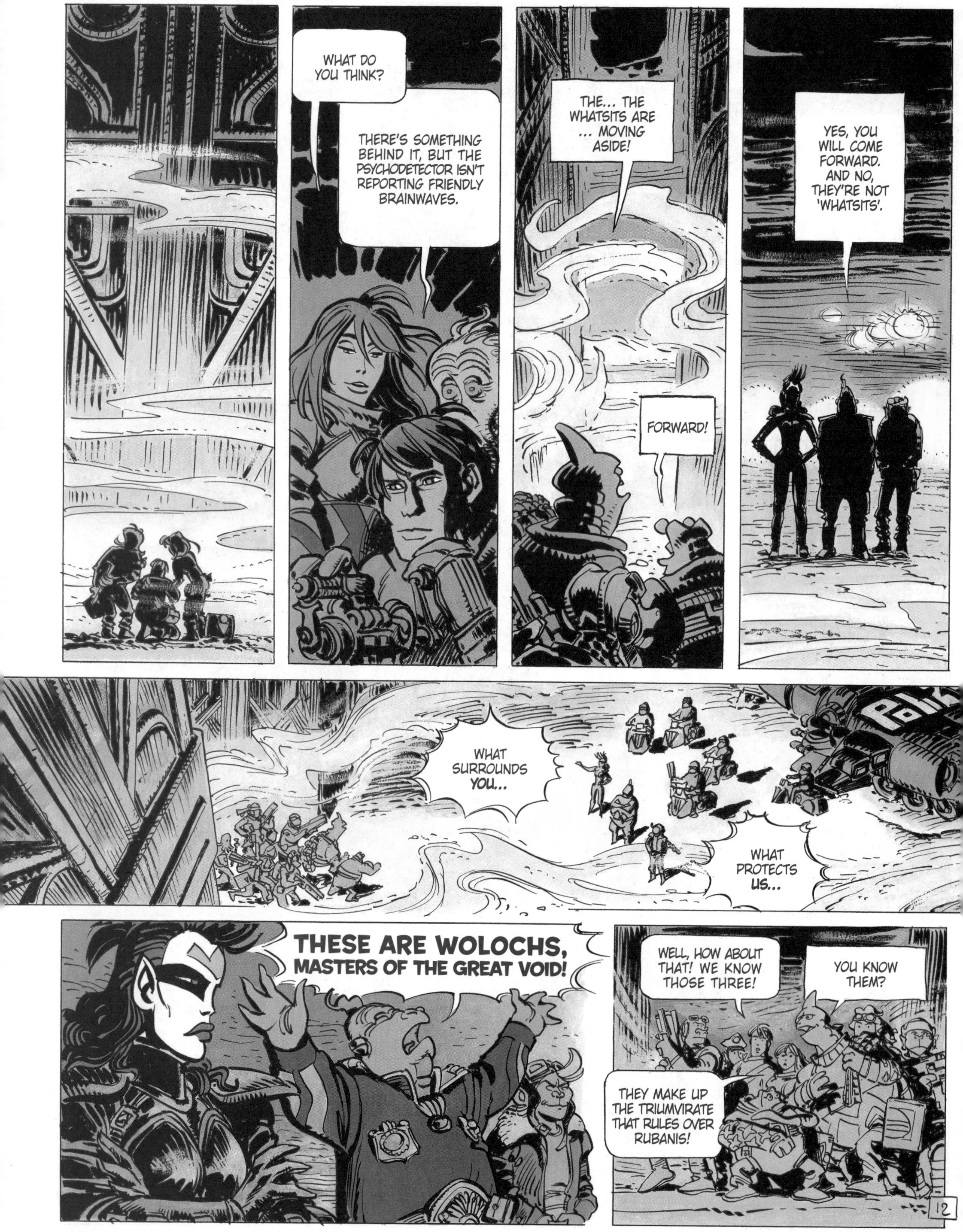
WHAT DO YOU THINK?
THERE'S SOMETHING BEHIND IT, BUT THE PSYCHODETECTOR ISN'T REPORTING FRIENDLY BRAINWAVES.
THE... THE WHATSITS ARE ... MOVING ASIDE!
FORWARD!
YES, YOU WILL COME FORWARD. AND NO, THEY'RE NOT 'WHATSITS'.
WHAT SURROUNDS YOU...
WHAT PROTECTS US...
THESE ARE WOLOCHS, MASTERS OF THE GREAT VOID!
WELL, HOW ABOUT THAT! WE KNOW THOSE THREE!
YOU KNOW THEM?
THEY MAKE UP THE TRIUMVIRATE THAT RULES OVER RUBANIS!
12

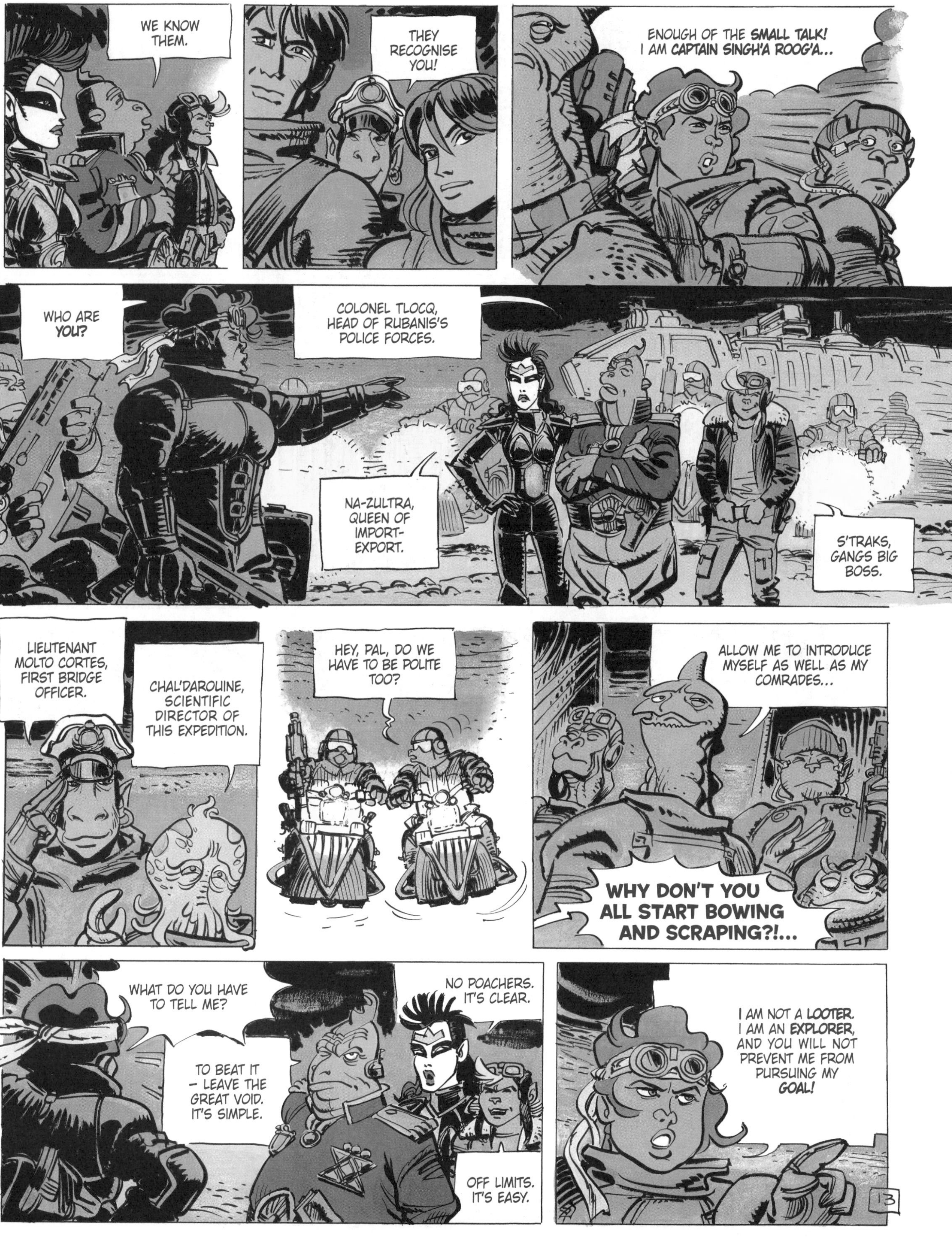
WE KNOW THEM.
THEY RECOGNISE YOU!
ENOUGH OF THE SMALL TALK! I AM CAPTAIN SINGH'A ROOG'A...
WHO ARE YOU?
COLONEL TLOCQ, HEAD OF RUBANIS'S POLICE FORCES.
NA-ZULTRA, QUEEN OF IMPORT-EXPORT.
S'TRAKS, GANGS BIG BOSS.
LIEUTENANT MOLTO CORTES, FIRST BRIDGE OFFICER.
CHAL'DAROUINE, SCIENTIFIC DIRECTOR OF THIS EXPEDITION.
HEY, PAL, DO WE HAVE TO BE POLITE TOO?
ALLOW ME TO INTRODUCE MYSELF AS WELL AS MY COMRADES...
WHY DON'T YOU ALL START BOWING AND SCRAPING?!...
WHAT DO YOU HAVE TO TELL ME?
TO BEAT IT – LEAVE THE GREAT VOID. IT'S SIMPLE.
NO POACHERS. IT'S CLEAR.
OFF LIMITS. IT'S EASY.
I AM NOT A LOOTER. I AM AN EXPLORER, AND YOU WILL NOT PREVENT ME FROM PURSUING MY GOAL!
13

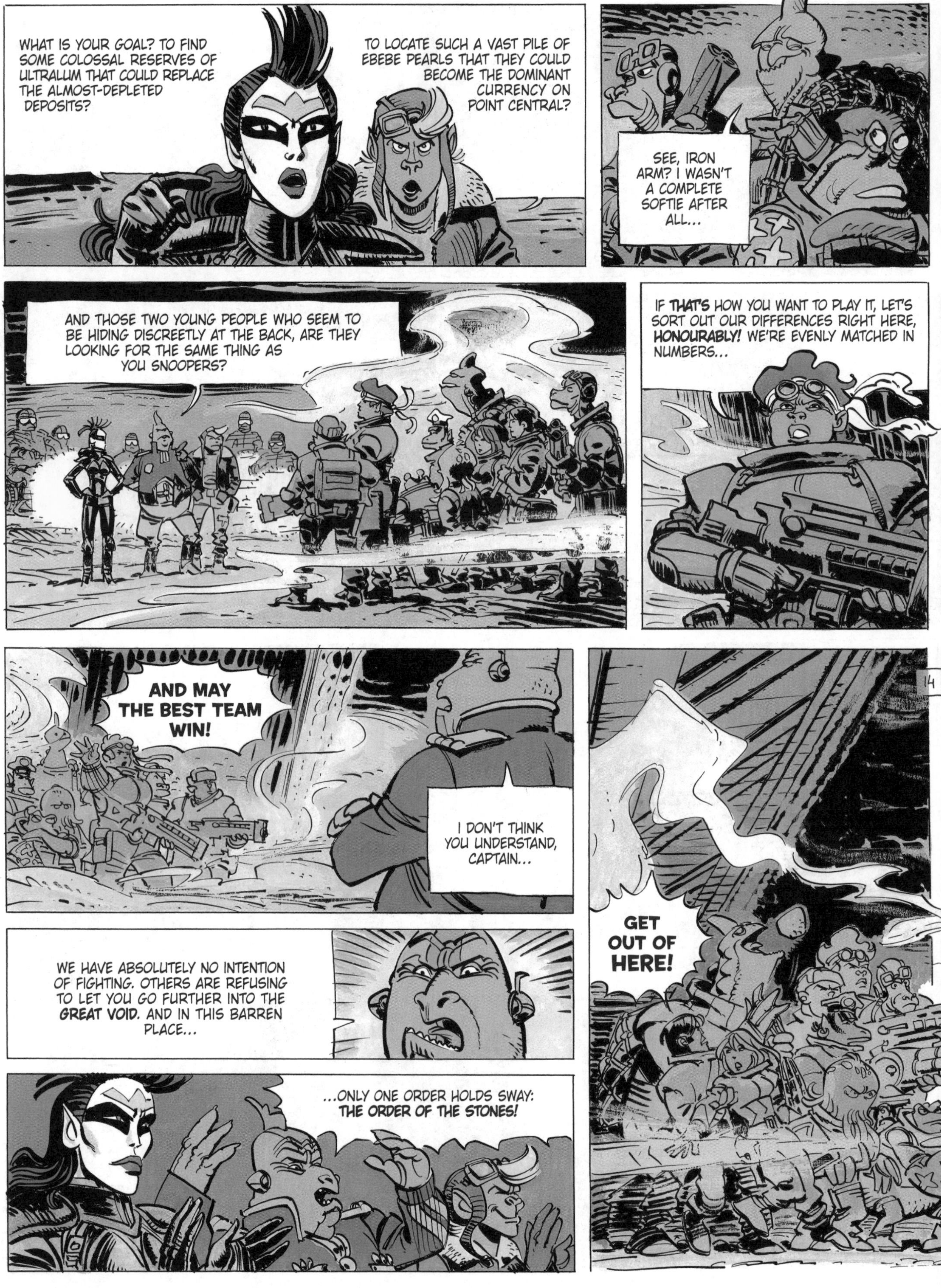

WHAT IS YOUR GOAL? TO FIND SOME COLOSSAL RESERVES OF ULTRALUM THAT COULD REPLACE THE ALMOST-DEPLETED DEPOSITS?
TO LOCATE SUCH A VAST PILE OF EBEBE PEARLS THAT THEY COULD BECOME THE DOMINANT CURRENCY ON POINT CENTRAL?
SEE, IRON ARM? I WASN'T A COMPLETE SOFTIE AFTER ALL...
AND THOSE TWO YOUNG PEOPLE WHO SEEM TO BE HIDING DISCREETLY AT THE BACK, ARE THEY LOOKING FOR THE SAME THING AS YOU SNOOPERS?
IF **THAT'S** HOW YOU WANT TO PLAY IT, LET'S SORT OUT OUR DIFFERENCES RIGHT HERE, **HONOURABLY!** WE'RE EVENLY MATCHED IN NUMBERS...
AND MAY THE BEST TEAM WIN!
I DON'T THINK YOU UNDERSTAND, CAPTAIN...
WE HAVE ABSOLUTELY NO INTENTION OF FIGHTING. OTHERS ARE REFUSING TO LET YOU GO FURTHER INTO THE **GREAT VOID.** AND IN THIS BARREN PLACE...
...ONLY ONE ORDER HOLDS SWAY: **THE ORDER OF THE STONES!**
GET OUT OF HERE!
14

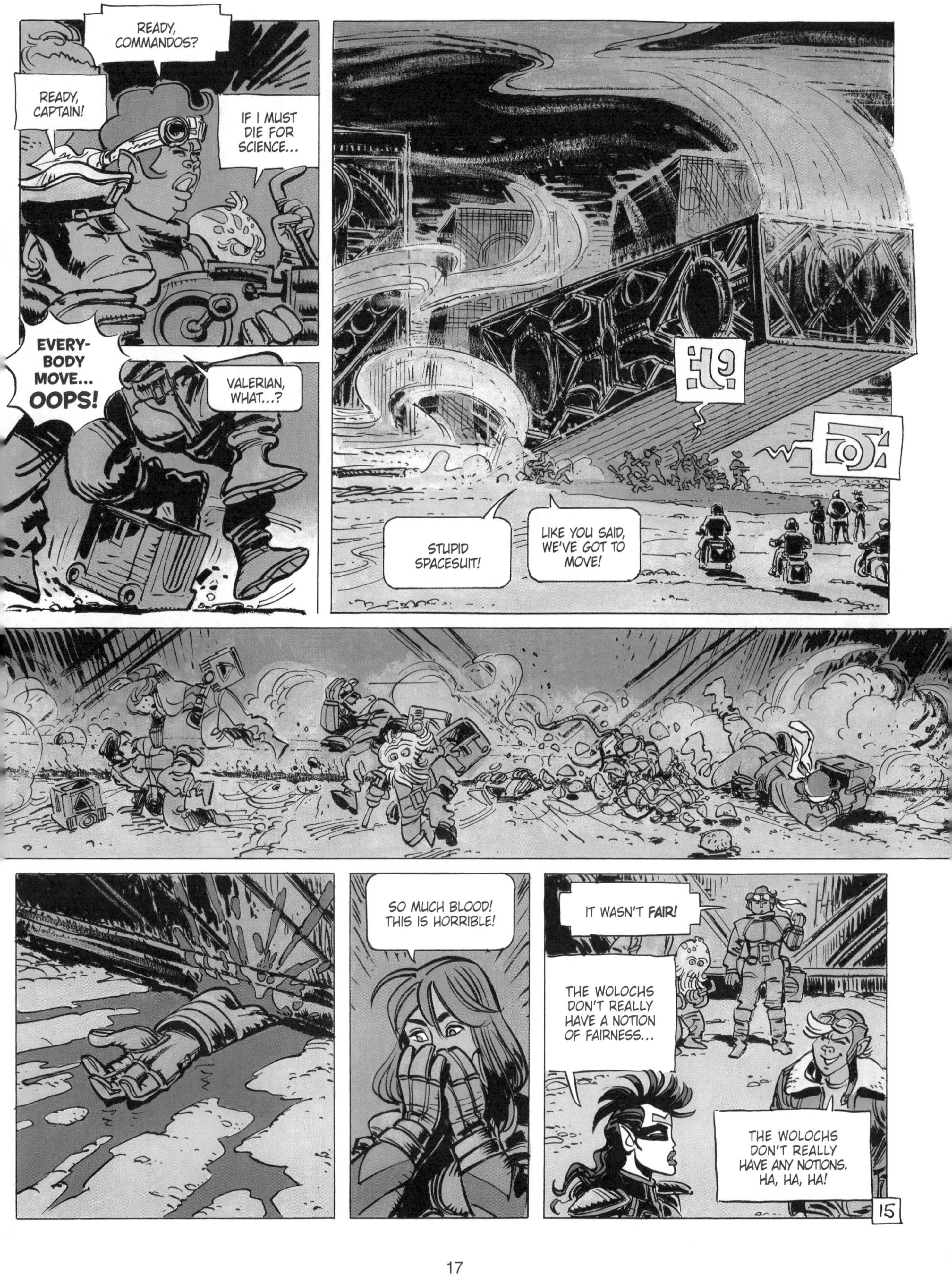
READY, COMMANDOS?
READY, CAPTAIN!
IF I MUST DIE FOR SCIENCE...
EVERY-BODY MOVE... **OOPS!**
VALERIAN, WHAT...?
STUPID SPACESUIT!
LIKE YOU SAID, WE'VE GOT TO MOVE!
SO MUCH BLOOD! THIS IS HORRIBLE!
IT WASN'T **FAIR!**
THE WOLOCHS DON'T REALLY HAVE A NOTION OF FAIRNESS...
THE WOLOCHS DON'T REALLY HAVE ANY NOTIONS. HA, HA, HA!
15

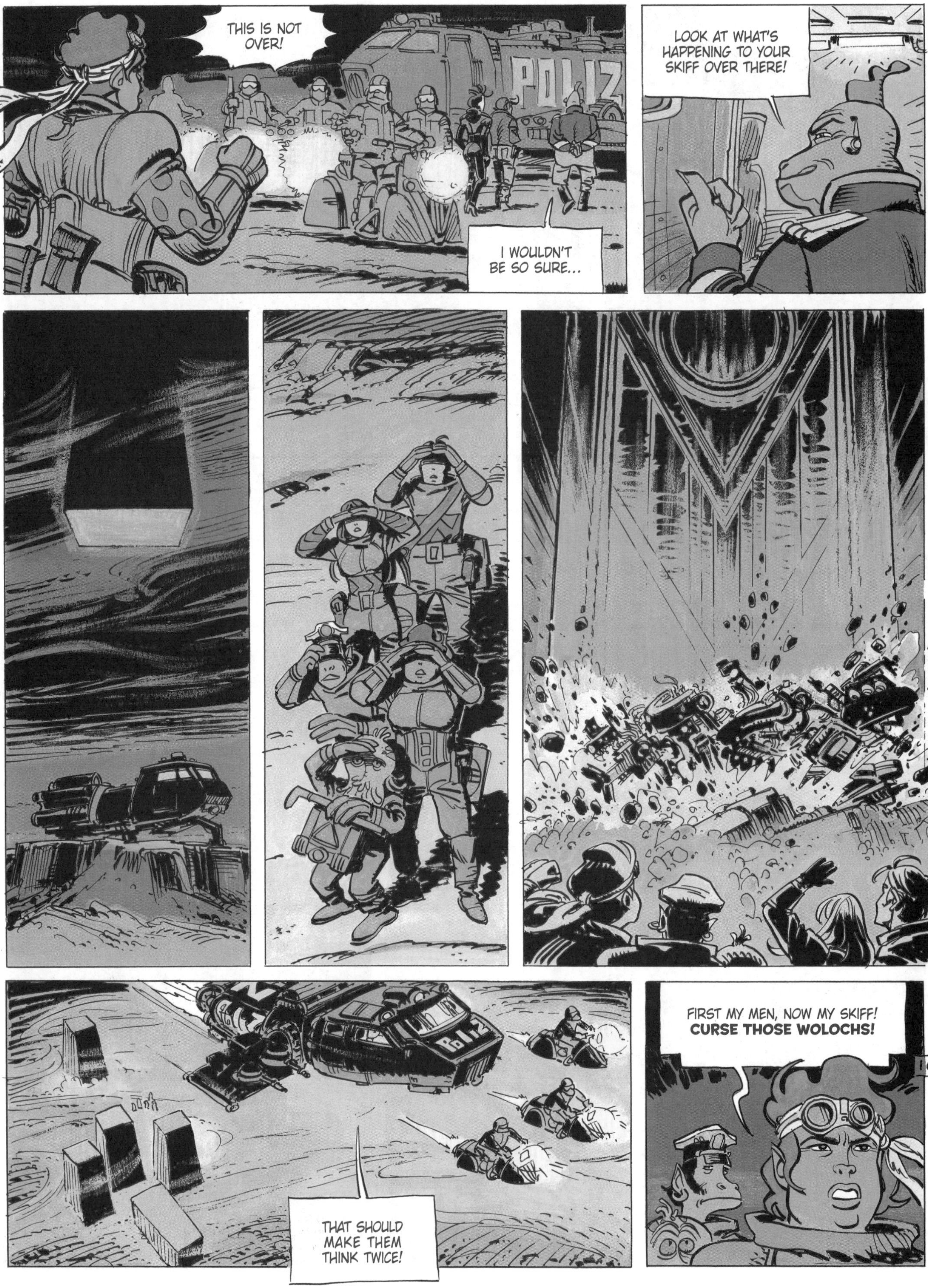
THIS IS NOT OVER!
I WOULDN'T BE SO SURE...
LOOK AT WHAT'S HAPPENING TO YOUR SKIFF OVER THERE!
THAT SHOULD MAKE THEM THINK TWICE!
FIRST MY MEN, NOW MY SKIFF! **CURSE THOSE WOLOCHS!**

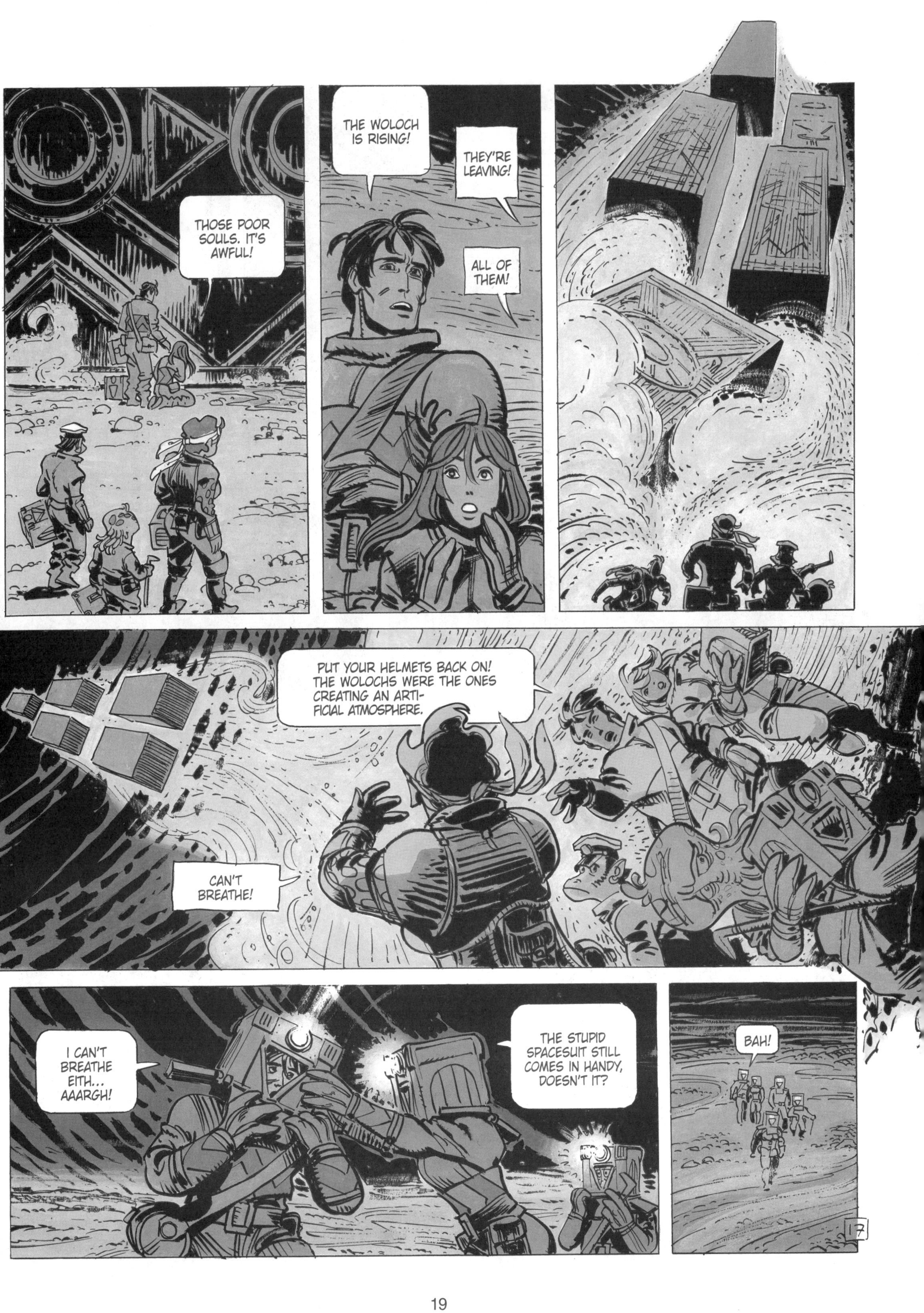
THOSE POOR SOULS. IT'S AWFUL!
THE WOLOCH IS RISING!
THEY'RE LEAVING!
ALL OF THEM!
PUT YOUR HELMETS BACK ON! THE WOLOCHS WERE THE ONES CREATING AN ARTI-FICIAL ATMOSPHERE.
CAN'T BREATHE!
I CAN'T BREATHE EITH... AAARGH!
THE STUPID SPACESUIT STILL COMES IN HANDY, DOESN'T IT?
BAH!
17

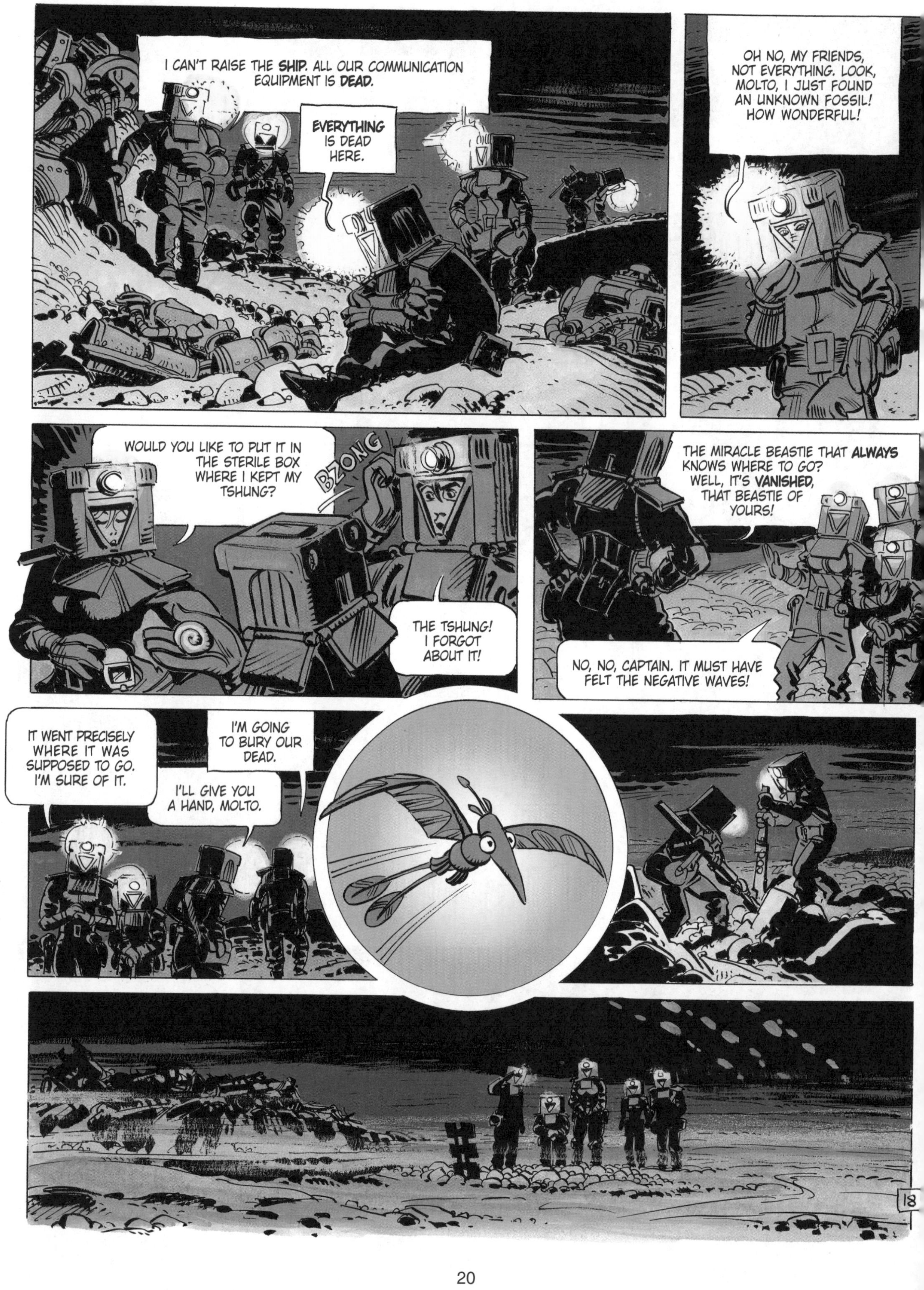

I CAN'T RAISE THE SHIP. ALL OUR COMMUNICATION EQUIPMENT IS DEAD.
EVERYTHING IS DEAD HERE.
OH NO, MY FRIENDS, NOT EVERYTHING. LOOK, MOLTO, I JUST FOUND AN UNKNOWN FOSSIL! HOW WONDERFUL!
WOULD YOU LIKE TO PUT IT IN THE STERILE BOX WHERE I KEPT MY TSHUNG?
BZONG
THE TSHUNG! I FORGOT ABOUT IT!
THE MIRACLE BEASTIE THAT ALWAYS KNOWS WHERE TO GO? WELL, IT'S VANISHED, THAT BEASTIE OF YOURS!
NO, NO, CAPTAIN. IT MUST HAVE FELT THE NEGATIVE WAVES!
IT WENT PRECISELY WHERE IT WAS SUPPOSED TO GO. I'M SURE OF IT.
I'M GOING TO BURY OUR DEAD.
I'LL GIVE YOU A HAND, MOLTO.
18

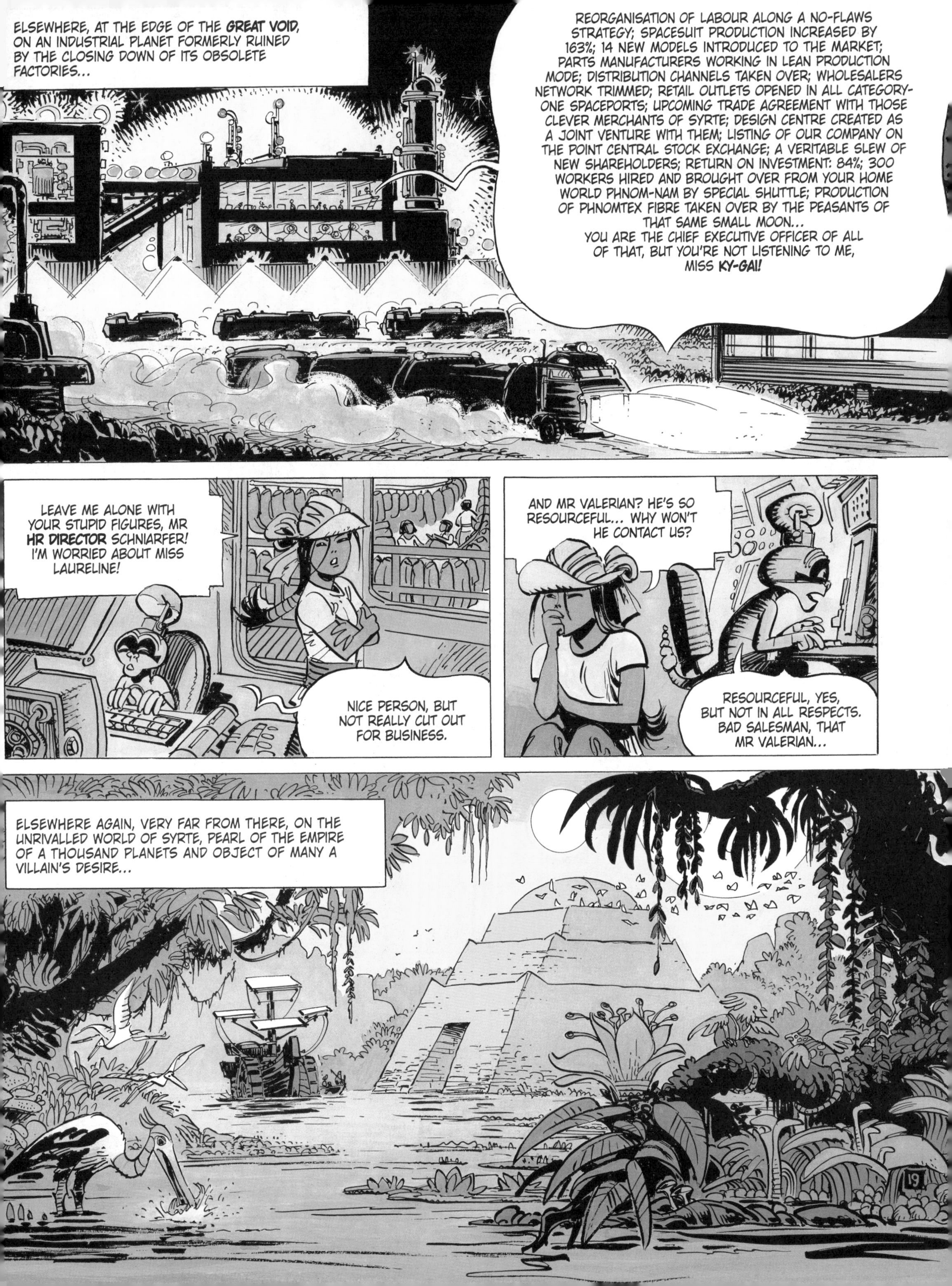
ELSEWHERE, AT THE EDGE OF THE **GREAT VOID**, ON AN INDUSTRIAL PLANET FORMERLY RUINED BY THE CLOSING DOWN OF ITS OBSOLETE FACTORIES...
REORGANISATION OF LABOUR ALONG A NO-FLAWS STRATEGY; SPACESUIT PRODUCTION INCREASED BY 163%; 14 NEW MODELS INTRODUCED TO THE MARKET; PARTS MANUFACTURERS WORKING IN LEAN PRODUCTION MODE; DISTRIBUTION CHANNELS TAKEN OVER; WHOLESALERS NETWORK TRIMMED; RETAIL OUTLETS OPENED IN ALL CATEGORY-ONE SPACEPORTS; UPCOMING TRADE AGREEMENT WITH THOSE CLEVER MERCHANTS OF SYRTE; DESIGN CENTRE CREATED AS A JOINT VENTURE WITH THEM; LISTING OF OUR COMPANY ON THE POINT CENTRAL STOCK EXCHANGE; A VERITABLE SLEW OF NEW SHAREHOLDERS; RETURN ON INVESTMENT: 84%; 300 WORKERS HIRED AND BROUGHT OVER FROM YOUR HOME WORLD PHNOM-NAM BY SPECIAL SHUTTLE; PRODUCTION OF PHNOMTEX FIBRE TAKEN OVER BY THE PEASANTS OF THAT SAME SMALL MOON... YOU ARE THE CHIEF EXECUTIVE OFFICER OF ALL OF THAT, BUT YOU'RE NOT LISTENING TO ME, MISS **KY-GAI!**
LEAVE ME ALONE WITH YOUR STUPID FIGURES, MR **HR DIRECTOR** SCHNIARFER! I'M WORRIED ABOUT MISS LAURELINE!
NICE PERSON, BUT NOT REALLY CUT OUT FOR BUSINESS.
AND MR VALERIAN? HE'S SO RESOURCEFUL... WHY WON'T HE CONTACT US?
RESOURCEFUL, YES, BUT NOT IN ALL RESPECTS. BAD SALESMAN, THAT MR VALERIAN...
ELSEWHERE AGAIN, VERY FAR FROM THERE, ON THE UNRIVALLED WORLD OF SYRTE, PEARL OF THE EMPIRE OF A THOUSAND PLANETS AND OBJECT OF MANY A VILLAIN'S DESIRE...
19

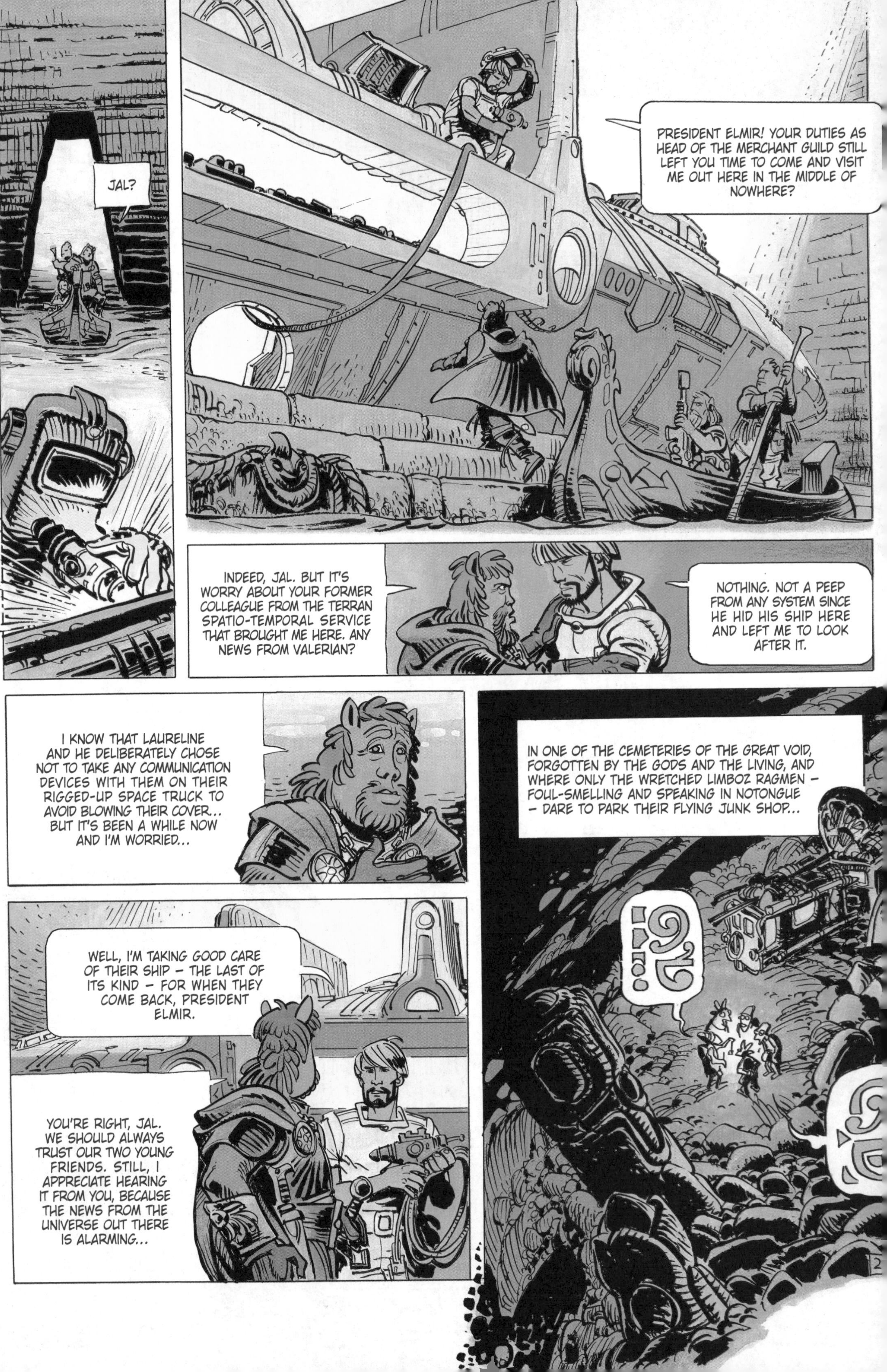

JAL?
PRESIDENT ELMIR! YOUR DUTIES AS HEAD OF THE MERCHANT GUILD STILL LEFT YOU TIME TO COME AND VISIT ME OUT HERE IN THE MIDDLE OF NOWHERE?
INDEED, JAL. BUT IT'S WORRY ABOUT YOUR FORMER COLLEAGUE FROM THE TERRAN SPATIO-TEMPORAL SERVICE THAT BROUGHT ME HERE. ANY NEWS FROM VALERIAN?
NOTHING. NOT A PEEP FROM ANY SYSTEM SINCE HE HID HIS SHIP HERE AND LEFT ME TO LOOK AFTER IT.
I KNOW THAT LAURELINE AND HE DELIBERATELY CHOSE NOT TO TAKE ANY COMMUNICATION DEVICES WITH THEM ON THEIR RIGGED-UP SPACE TRUCK TO AVOID BLOWING THEIR COVER... BUT IT'S BEEN A WHILE NOW AND I'M WORRIED...
WELL, I'M TAKING GOOD CARE OF THEIR SHIP – THE LAST OF ITS KIND – FOR WHEN THEY COME BACK, PRESIDENT ELMIR.
YOU'RE RIGHT, JAL. WE SHOULD ALWAYS TRUST OUR TWO YOUNG FRIENDS. STILL, I APPRECIATE HEARING IT FROM YOU, BECAUSE THE NEWS FROM THE UNIVERSE OUT THERE IS ALARMING...
IN ONE OF THE CEMETERIES OF THE GREAT VOID, FORGOTTEN BY THE GODS AND THE LIVING, AND WHERE ONLY THE WRETCHED LIMBOZ RAGMEN – FOUL-SMELLING AND SPEAKING IN NOTONGUE – DARE TO PARK THEIR FLYING JUNK SHOP...

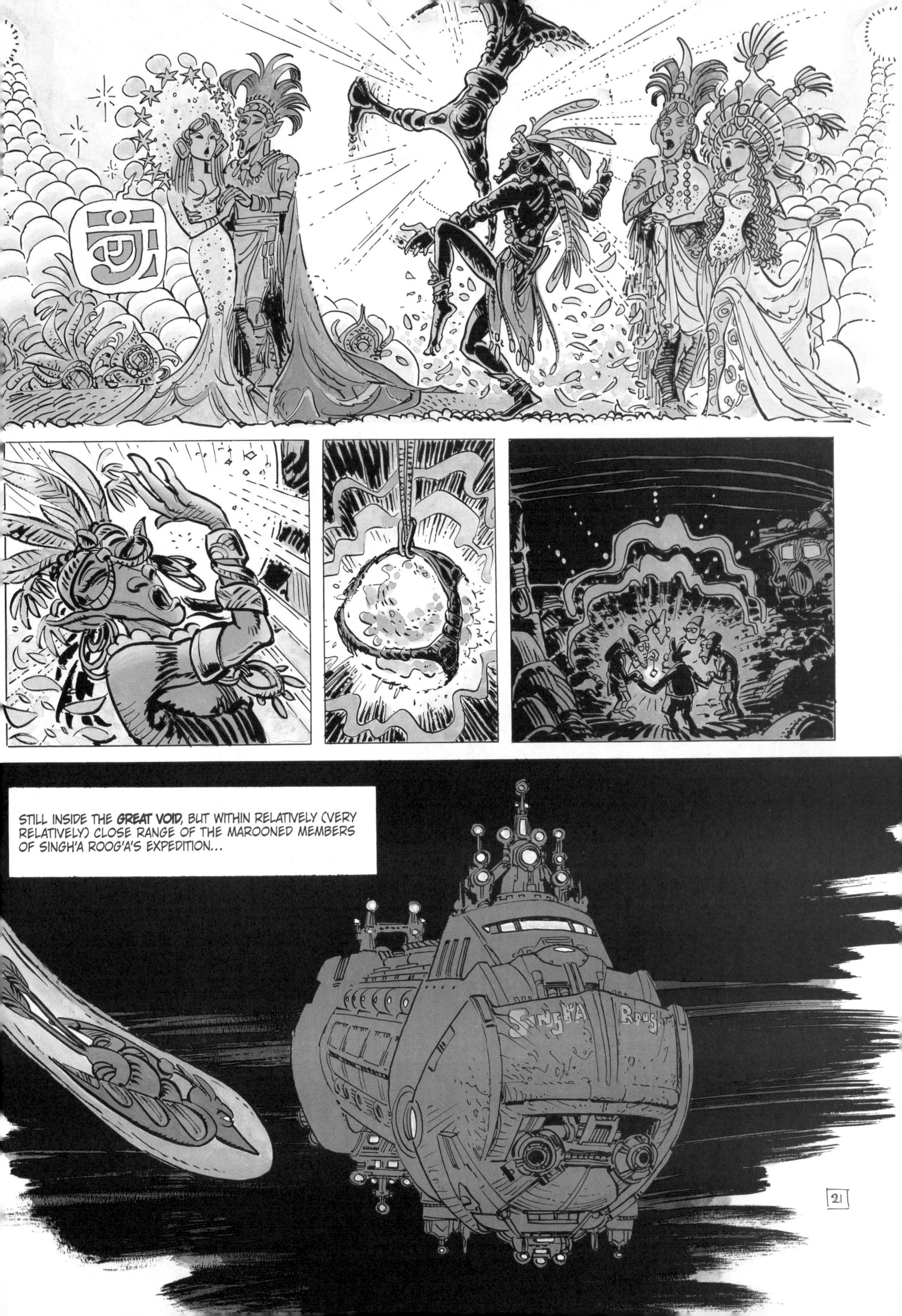
STILL INSIDE THE **GREAT VOID**, BUT WITHIN RELATIVELY (VERY RELATIVELY) CLOSE RANGE OF THE MAROONED MEMBERS OF SINGH'A ROOG'A'S EXPEDITION...

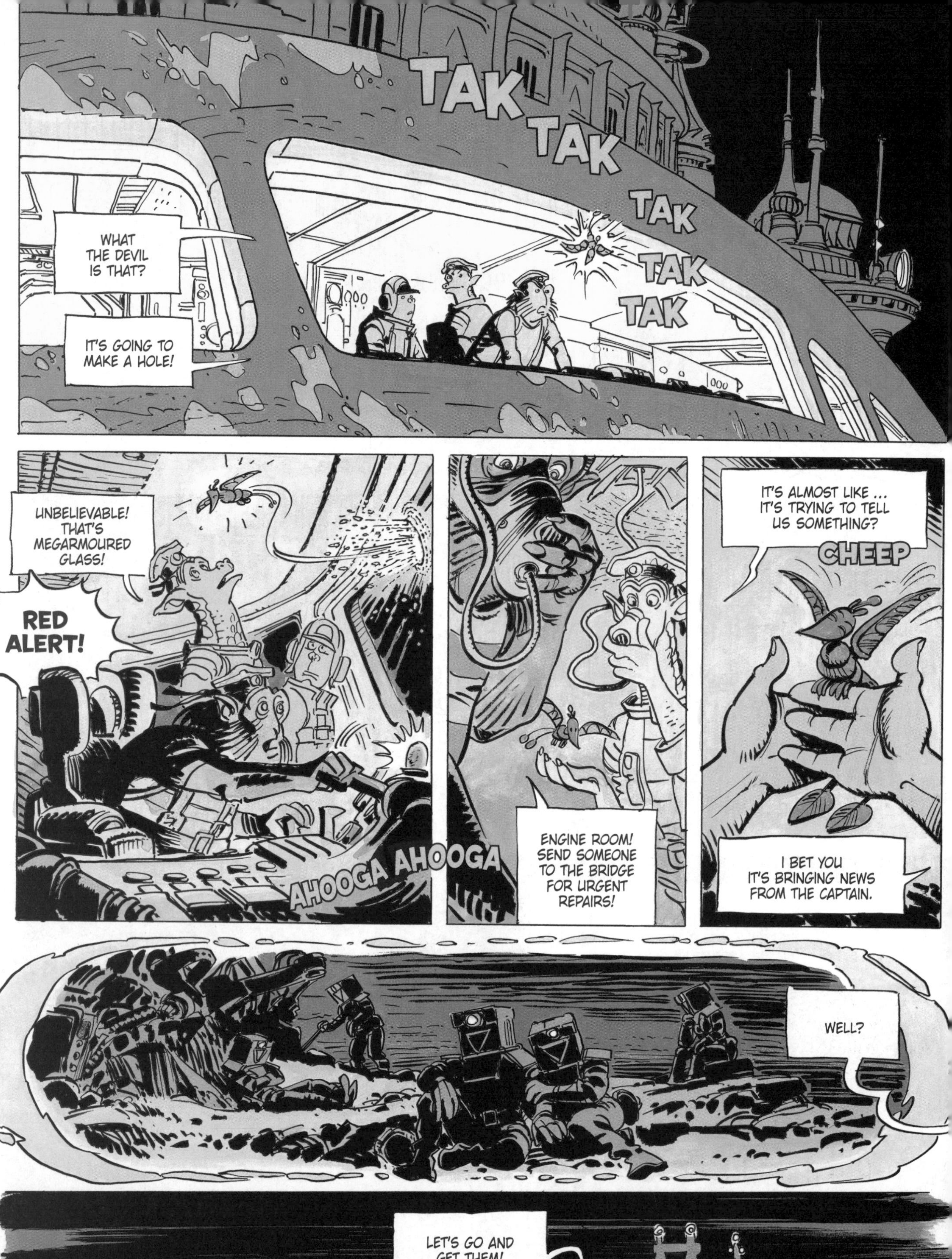
TAK
TAK
TAK
TAK
TAK
WHAT THE DEVIL IS THAT?
IT'S GOING TO MAKE A HOLE!
UNBELIEVABLE! THAT'S MEGARMOURED GLASS!
RED ALERT!
AHOOGA AHOOGA
ENGINE ROOM! SEND SOMEONE TO THE BRIDGE FOR URGENT REPAIRS!
IT'S ALMOST LIKE ... IT'S TRYING TO TELL US SOMETHING?
CHEEP
I BET YOU IT'S BRINGING NEWS FROM THE CAPTAIN.
WELL?
LET'S GO AND GET THEM!
22

SOMEWHERE IN THE NOTHING-AT-ALL OF THE **GREAT VOID**, WHERE THE MATTER OF THE FORMING UNIVERSE ROARS SILENTLY, WHERE THE SHAPELESS EDDIES OF TIME WHIRL MADLY, WHERE DARK ENERGY GIVES BIRTH TO STONE MONSTERS...

IS OUR WOLOCH MASTER HAPPY?

WOLOCHS DO NOT HAVE FEELINGS, COLONEL TLOCQ.

SATISFIED, THEN?

WOLOCHS HAVE NO MEASURABLE CRITERIA, TRIUMVIR NA ZULTRA.

DID WE DO WHAT IT WANTED OR NOT?

THE WOLOCHS DON'T WANT ANYTHING TO STAND IN THEIR WAY. ANYTHING THAT MIGHT BE A HINDRANCE MUST BE DESTROYED. THE WOLOCHS NEED NOTHING, NO ONE. THEY ARE THEIR OWN POWER SOURCE; THEY ARE THEIR OWN SPACE VEHICLE; THEY ARE THEIR OWN WEAPON OF MASS DESTRUCTION.

NO NEED FOR HOSTILITY, TRIUMVIR S'TRAKS. MUST I REMIND YOU THAT THE WOLOCHS CAN UTTERLY DESTROY YOU?...

WHY WOULD THEY, THOUGH?

23

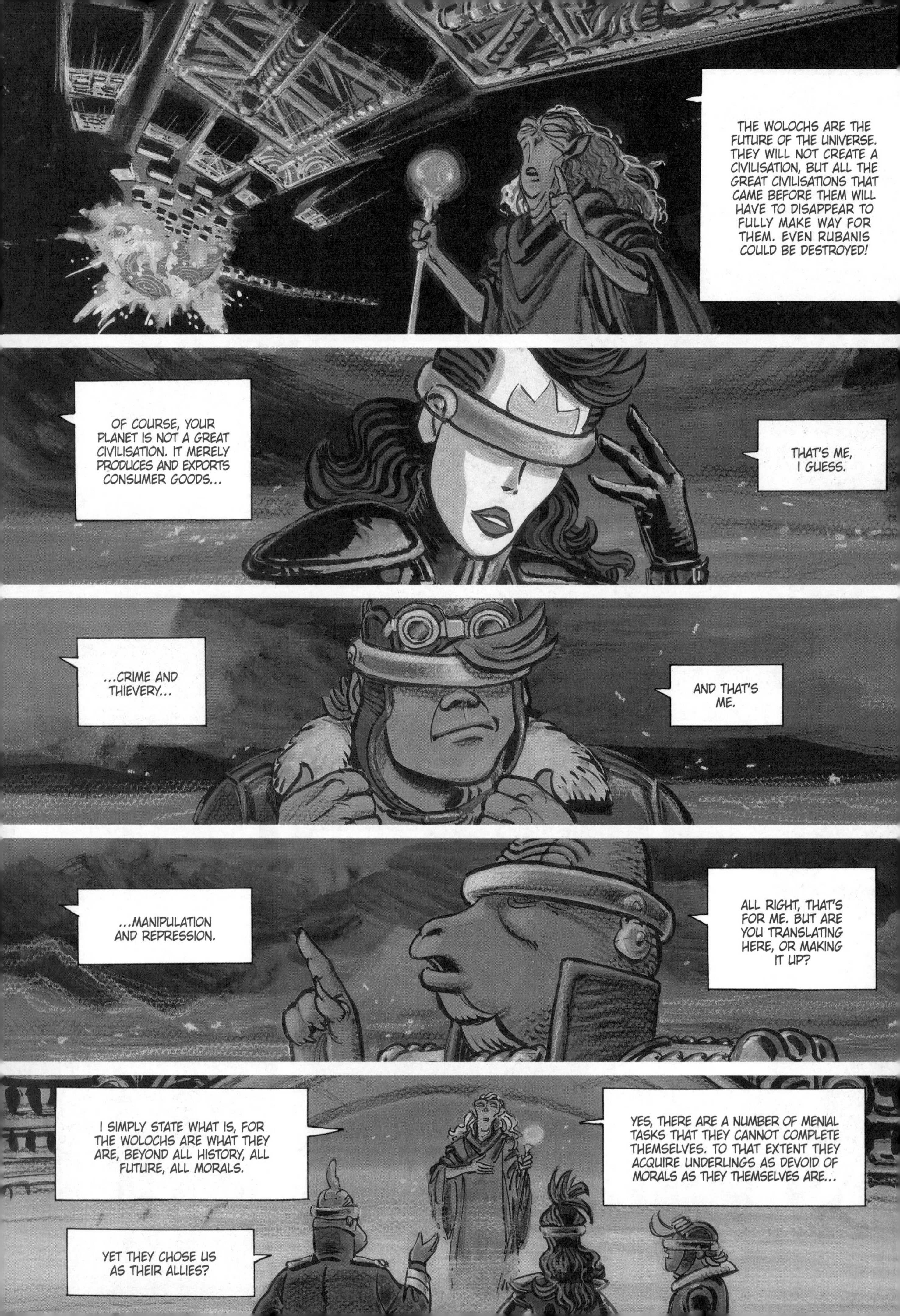
THE WOLOCHS ARE THE FUTURE OF THE UNIVERSE. THEY WILL NOT CREATE A CIVILISATION, BUT ALL THE GREAT CIVILISATIONS THAT CAME BEFORE THEM WILL HAVE TO DISAPPEAR TO FULLY MAKE WAY FOR THEM. EVEN RUBANIS COULD BE DESTROYED!
OF COURSE, YOUR PLANET IS NOT A GREAT CIVILISATION. IT MERELY PRODUCES AND EXPORTS CONSUMER GOODS...
THAT'S ME, I GUESS.
...CRIME AND THIEVERY...
AND THAT'S ME.
...MANIPULATION AND REPRESSION.
ALL RIGHT, THAT'S FOR ME. BUT ARE YOU TRANSLATING HERE, OR MAKING IT UP?
I SIMPLY STATE WHAT IS, FOR THE WOLOCHS ARE WHAT THEY ARE, BEYOND ALL HISTORY, ALL FUTURE, ALL MORALS.
YET THEY CHOSE US AS THEIR ALLIES?
YES, THERE ARE A NUMBER OF MENIAL TASKS THAT THEY CANNOT COMPLETE THEMSELVES. TO THAT EXTENT THEY ACQUIRE UNDERLINGS AS DEVOID OF MORALS AS THEY THEMSELVES ARE...

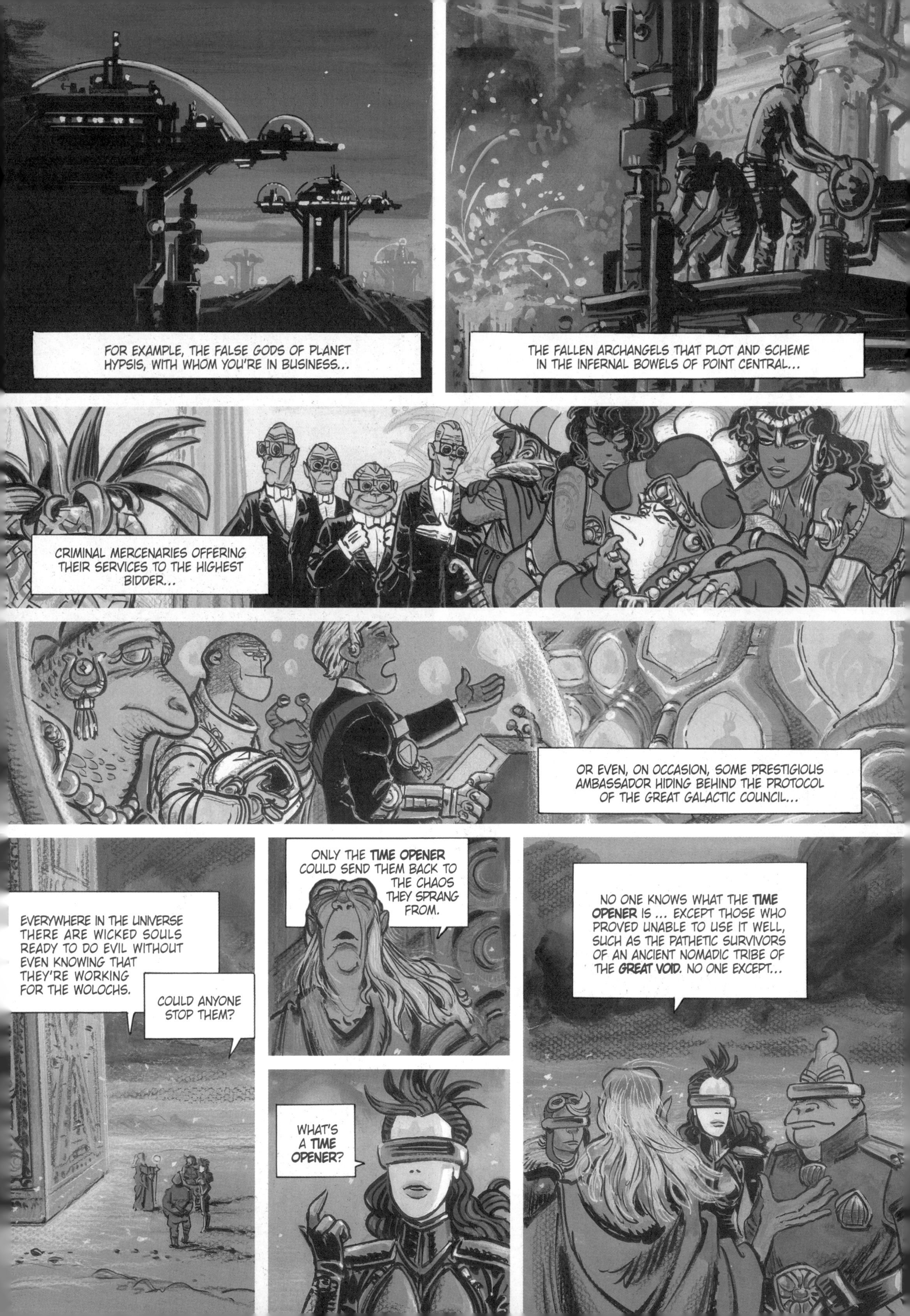

FOR EXAMPLE, THE FALSE GODS OF PLANET HYPSIS, WITH WHOM YOU'RE IN BUSINESS...
THE FALLEN ARCHANGELS THAT PLOT AND SCHEME IN THE INFERNAL BOWELS OF POINT CENTRAL...
CRIMINAL MERCENARIES OFFERING THEIR SERVICES TO THE HIGHEST BIDDER...
OR EVEN, ON OCCASION, SOME PRESTIGIOUS AMBASSADOR HIDING BEHIND THE PROTOCOL OF THE GREAT GALACTIC COUNCIL...
EVERYWHERE IN THE UNIVERSE THERE ARE WICKED SOULS READY TO DO EVIL WITHOUT EVEN KNOWING THAT THEY'RE WORKING FOR THE WOLOCHS.
COULD ANYONE STOP THEM?
ONLY THE **TIME OPENER** COULD SEND THEM BACK TO THE CHAOS THEY SPRANG FROM.
WHAT'S A **TIME OPENER**?
NO ONE KNOWS WHAT THE **TIME OPENER** IS ... EXCEPT THOSE WHO PROVED UNABLE TO USE IT WELL, SUCH AS THE PATHETIC SURVIVORS OF AN ANCIENT NOMADIC TRIBE OF THE **GREAT VOID**. NO ONE EXCEPT...

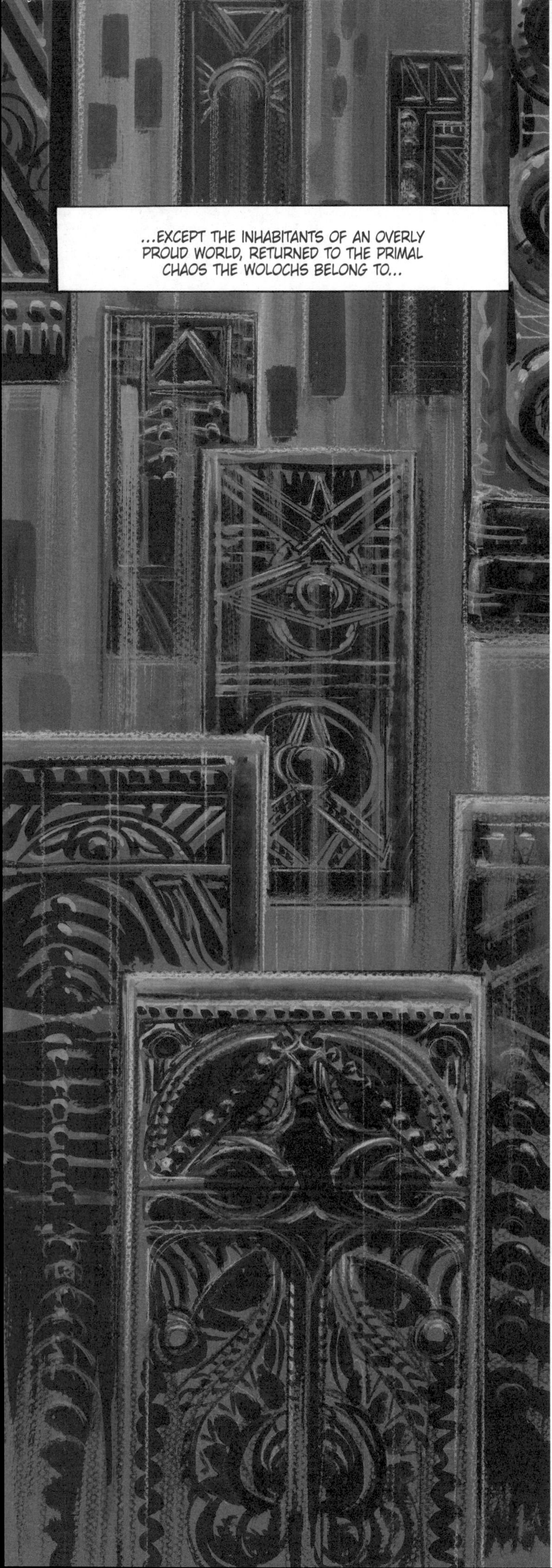
...EXCEPT THE INHABITANTS OF AN OVERLY PROUD WORLD, RETURNED TO THE PRIMAL CHAOS THE WOLOCHS BELONG TO...

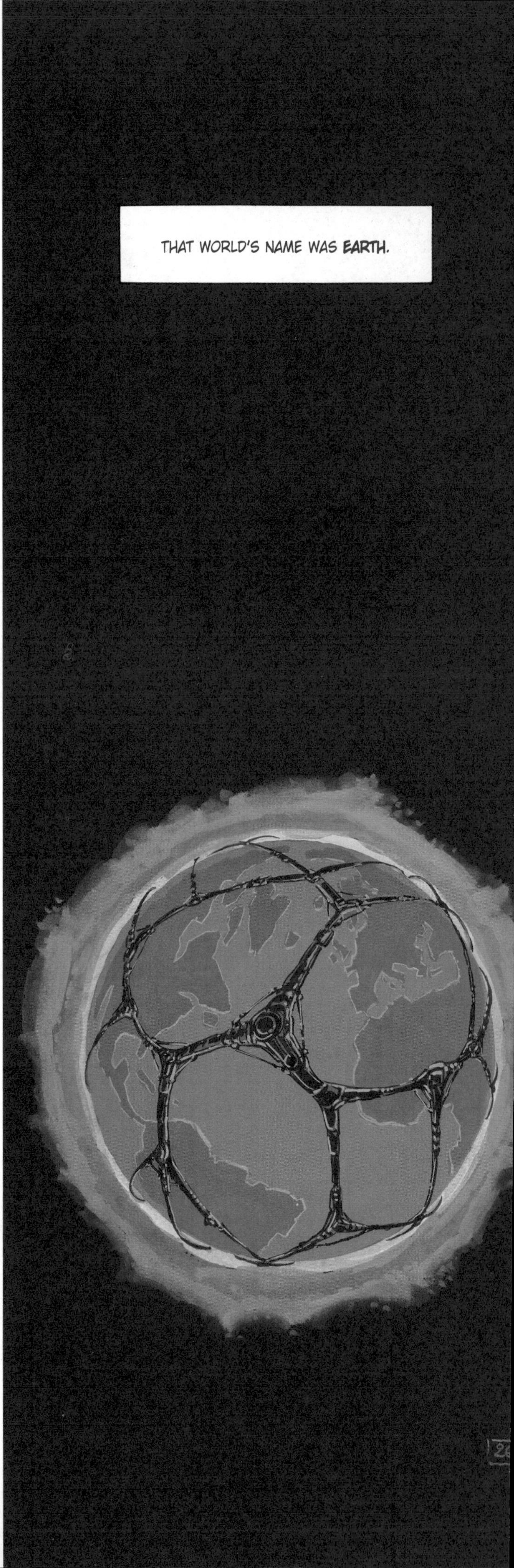
THAT WORLD'S NAME WAS **EARTH**.

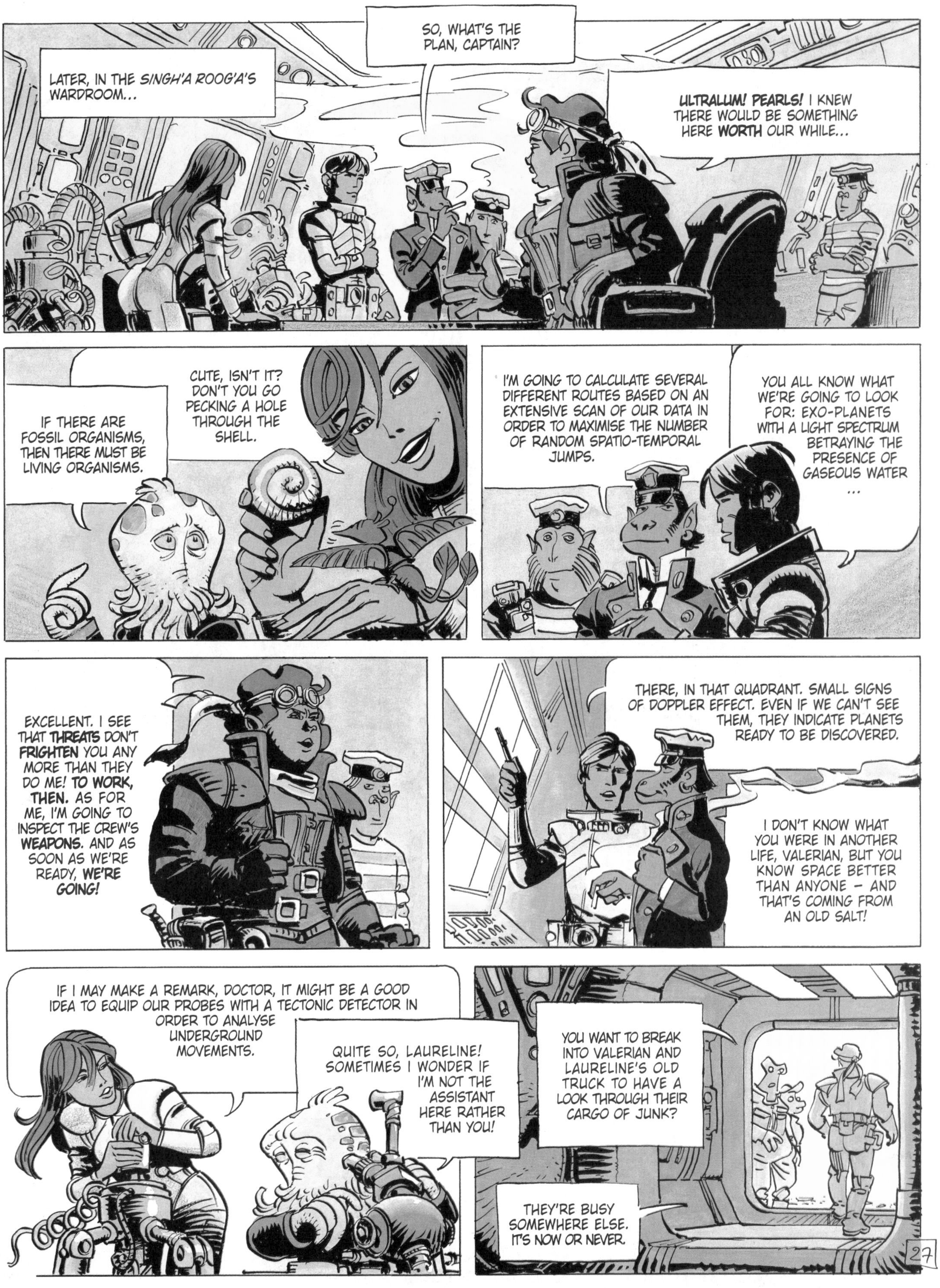
LATER, IN THE *SINGH'A ROOG'A'S* WARDROOM...
SO, WHAT'S THE PLAN, CAPTAIN?
ULTRALUM! PEARLS! I KNEW THERE WOULD BE SOMETHING HERE **WORTH** OUR WHILE...
IF THERE ARE FOSSIL ORGANISMS, THEN THERE MUST BE LIVING ORGANISMS.
CUTE, ISN'T IT? DON'T YOU GO PECKING A HOLE THROUGH THE SHELL.
I'M GOING TO CALCULATE SEVERAL DIFFERENT ROUTES BASED ON AN EXTENSIVE SCAN OF OUR DATA IN ORDER TO MAXIMISE THE NUMBER OF RANDOM SPATIO-TEMPORAL JUMPS.
YOU ALL KNOW WHAT WE'RE GOING TO LOOK FOR: EXO-PLANETS WITH A LIGHT SPECTRUM BETRAYING THE PRESENCE OF GASEOUS WATER ...
EXCELLENT. I SEE THAT **THREATS** DON'T **FRIGHTEN** YOU ANY MORE THAN THEY DO ME! **TO WORK, THEN.** AS FOR ME, I'M GOING TO INSPECT THE CREW'S **WEAPONS.** AND AS SOON AS WE'RE READY, **WE'RE GOING!**
THERE, IN THAT QUADRANT. SMALL SIGNS OF DOPPLER EFFECT. EVEN IF WE CAN'T SEE THEM, THEY INDICATE PLANETS READY TO BE DISCOVERED.
I DON'T KNOW WHAT YOU WERE IN ANOTHER LIFE, VALERIAN, BUT YOU KNOW SPACE BETTER THAN ANYONE – AND THAT'S COMING FROM AN OLD SALT!
IF I MAY MAKE A REMARK, DOCTOR, IT MIGHT BE A GOOD IDEA TO EQUIP OUR PROBES WITH A TECTONIC DETECTOR IN ORDER TO ANALYSE UNDERGROUND MOVEMENTS.
QUITE SO, LAURELINE! SOMETIMES I WONDER IF I'M NOT THE ASSISTANT HERE RATHER THAN YOU!
YOU WANT TO BREAK INTO VALERIAN AND LAURELINE'S OLD TRUCK TO HAVE A LOOK THROUGH THEIR CARGO OF JUNK?
THEY'RE BUSY SOMEWHERE ELSE. IT'S NOW OR NEVER.
27

I'M NOT SO SURE IT'S ALL JUST JUNK IN THERE. THOSE UNIROOS STANDING GUARD, FOR EXAMPLE? I KNOW HOW EFFECTIVE THEY ARE...

BZOING   BZOING

READY FOR THE FIRST BIG JUMP? I'M GOING BACK TO THE BRIDGE.

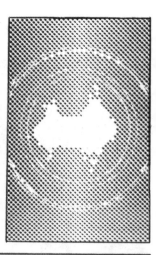

AT ABOUT THE SAME TIME, ON THE ENORMOUS PLANET RUBANIS, WHERE CONFLICTS OF INTEREST ARE STILL RAGING UNREMITTINGLY...

SO, TRIUMVIRS, WHY DO YOU THINK THE TRANSLATOR TOLD US ABOUT THAT **TIME OPENER** THING, HUH?

SO THAT WE'LL LOOK FOR IT FOR THEM, BECAUSE WE'RE BETTER EQUIPPED TO DO SO.

SO THAT WE'LL FIND IT AND KEEP IT FOR OURSELVES! HA, HA, HA!

VERY GOOD. BUT WHAT ABOUT US? WHY DID WE MENTION ULTRALLUM AND PEARLS TO THE BIG CAPTAIN?

SO THAT SHE'LL LOOK FOR THEM FOR US, BECAUSE HER EXPEDITION'S BETTER EQUIPPED TO DO SO.

AND SO THAT WE'LL KEEP THEM FOR OURSELVES ONCE SHE'S FOUND THEM! HA, HA, HA!

STILL VERY GOOD. BUT WHAT HAVE WE DECIDED TO DO ONCE SHE'S FOUND THEM?

TO TAKE OUT THE *SINGH'A ROOG'A* WITH THE WOLOCHS' HELP.

A BIG BOOM IN THE SILENCE OF THE GREAT VOID, THEN BRING ON THE PEARLS AND THE ULTRALLUM!

VERY, VERY GOOD. SO, WHAT DO YOU THINK THE WOLOCHS WILL DO WITH US ONCE WE'VE FOUND THE **TIME OPENER?**

AH...

UNCOOL...

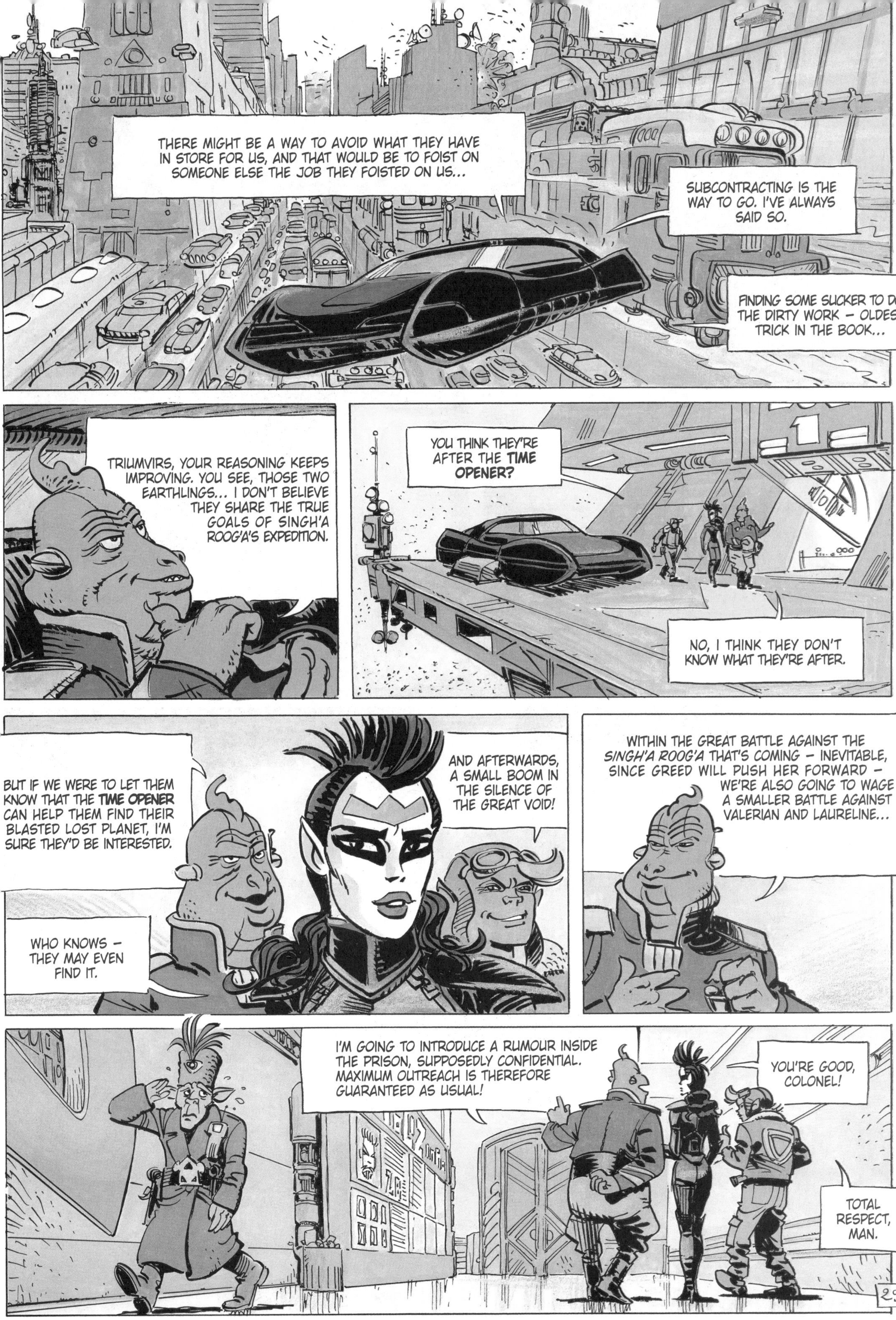
THERE MIGHT BE A WAY TO AVOID WHAT THEY HAVE IN STORE FOR US, AND THAT WOULD BE TO FOIST ON SOMEONE ELSE THE JOB THEY FOISTED ON US...
SUBCONTRACTING IS THE WAY TO GO. I'VE ALWAYS SAID SO.
FINDING SOME SUCKER TO DO THE DIRTY WORK – OLDEST TRICK IN THE BOOK...
TRIUMVIRS, YOUR REASONING KEEPS IMPROVING. YOU SEE, THOSE TWO EARTHLINGS... I DON'T BELIEVE THEY SHARE THE TRUE GOALS OF SINGH'A ROOG'A'S EXPEDITION.
YOU THINK THEY'RE AFTER THE **TIME OPENER?**
NO, I THINK THEY DON'T KNOW WHAT THEY'RE AFTER.
BUT IF WE WERE TO LET THEM KNOW THAT THE **TIME OPENER** CAN HELP THEM FIND THEIR BLASTED LOST PLANET, I'M SURE THEY'D BE INTERESTED.
WHO KNOWS – THEY MAY EVEN FIND IT.
AND AFTERWARDS, A SMALL BOOM IN THE SILENCE OF THE GREAT VOID!
WITHIN THE GREAT BATTLE AGAINST THE *SINGH'A ROOG'A* THAT'S COMING – INEVITABLE, SINCE GREED WILL PUSH HER FORWARD – WE'RE ALSO GOING TO WAGE A SMALLER BATTLE AGAINST VALERIAN AND LAURELINE...
I'M GOING TO INTRODUCE A RUMOUR INSIDE THE PRISON, SUPPOSEDLY CONFIDENTIAL. MAXIMUM OUTREACH IS THEREFORE GUARANTEED AS USUAL!
YOU'RE GOOD, COLONEL!
TOTAL RESPECT, MAN.
29

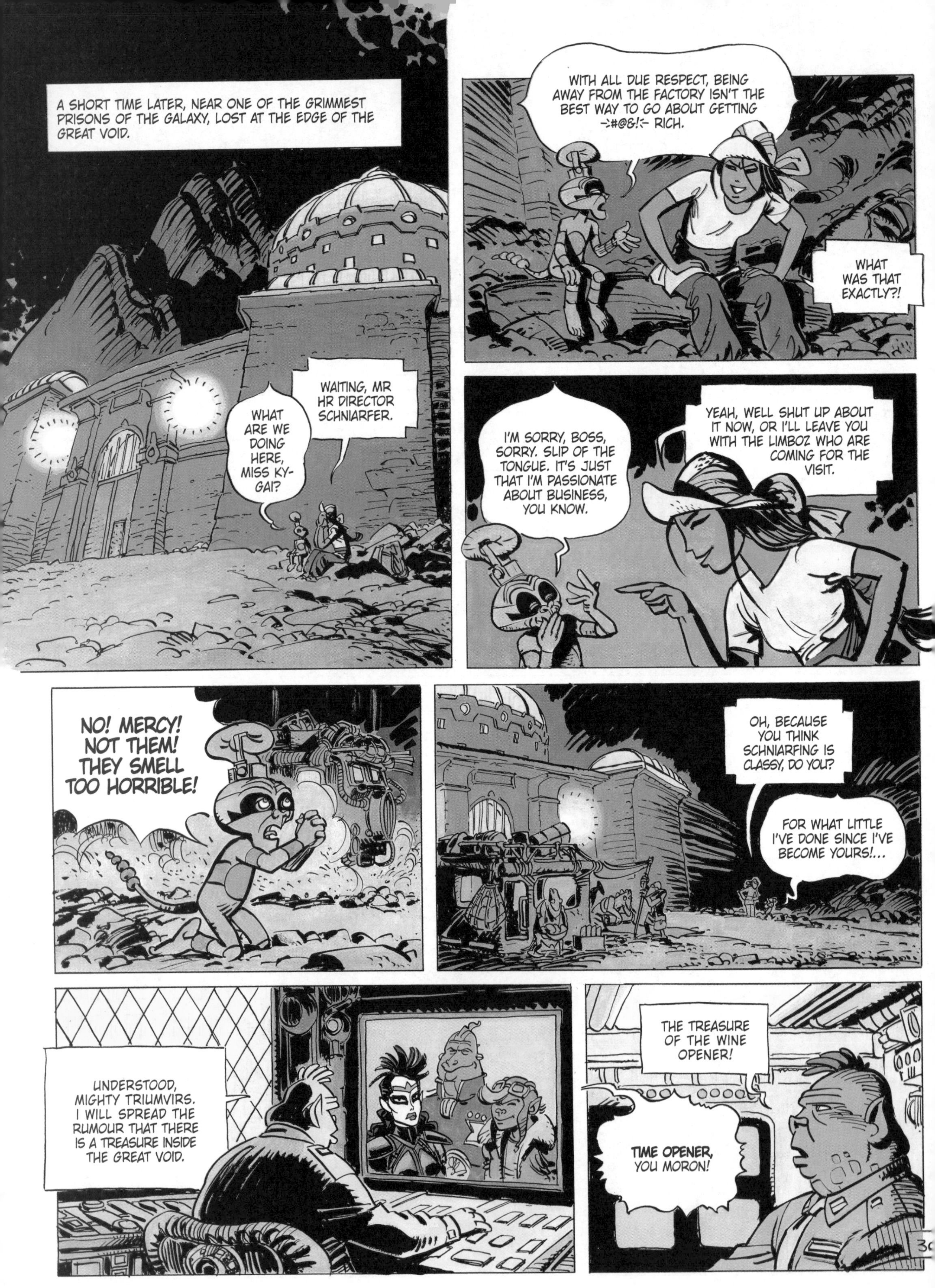
A SHORT TIME LATER, NEAR ONE OF THE GRIMMEST PRISONS OF THE GALAXY, LOST AT THE EDGE OF THE GREAT VOID.
WHAT ARE WE DOING HERE, MISS KY-GAI?
WAITING, MR HR DIRECTOR SCHNIARFER.
WITH ALL DUE RESPECT, BEING AWAY FROM THE FACTORY ISN'T THE BEST WAY TO GO ABOUT GETTING -#@&!- RICH.
WHAT WAS THAT EXACTLY?!
I'M SORRY, BOSS, SORRY. SLIP OF THE TONGUE. IT'S JUST THAT I'M PASSIONATE ABOUT BUSINESS, YOU KNOW.
YEAH, WELL SHUT UP ABOUT IT NOW, OR I'LL LEAVE YOU WITH THE LIMBOZ WHO ARE COMING FOR THE VISIT.
NO! MERCY! NOT THEM! THEY SMELL TOO HORRIBLE!
OH, BECAUSE YOU THINK SCHNIARFING IS CLASSY, DO YOU?
FOR WHAT LITTLE I'VE DONE SINCE I'VE BECOME YOURS!...
UNDERSTOOD, MIGHTY TRIUMVIRS. I WILL SPREAD THE RUMOUR THAT THERE IS A TREASURE INSIDE THE GREAT VOID.
THE TREASURE OF THE WINE OPENER!
TIME OPENER, YOU MORON!

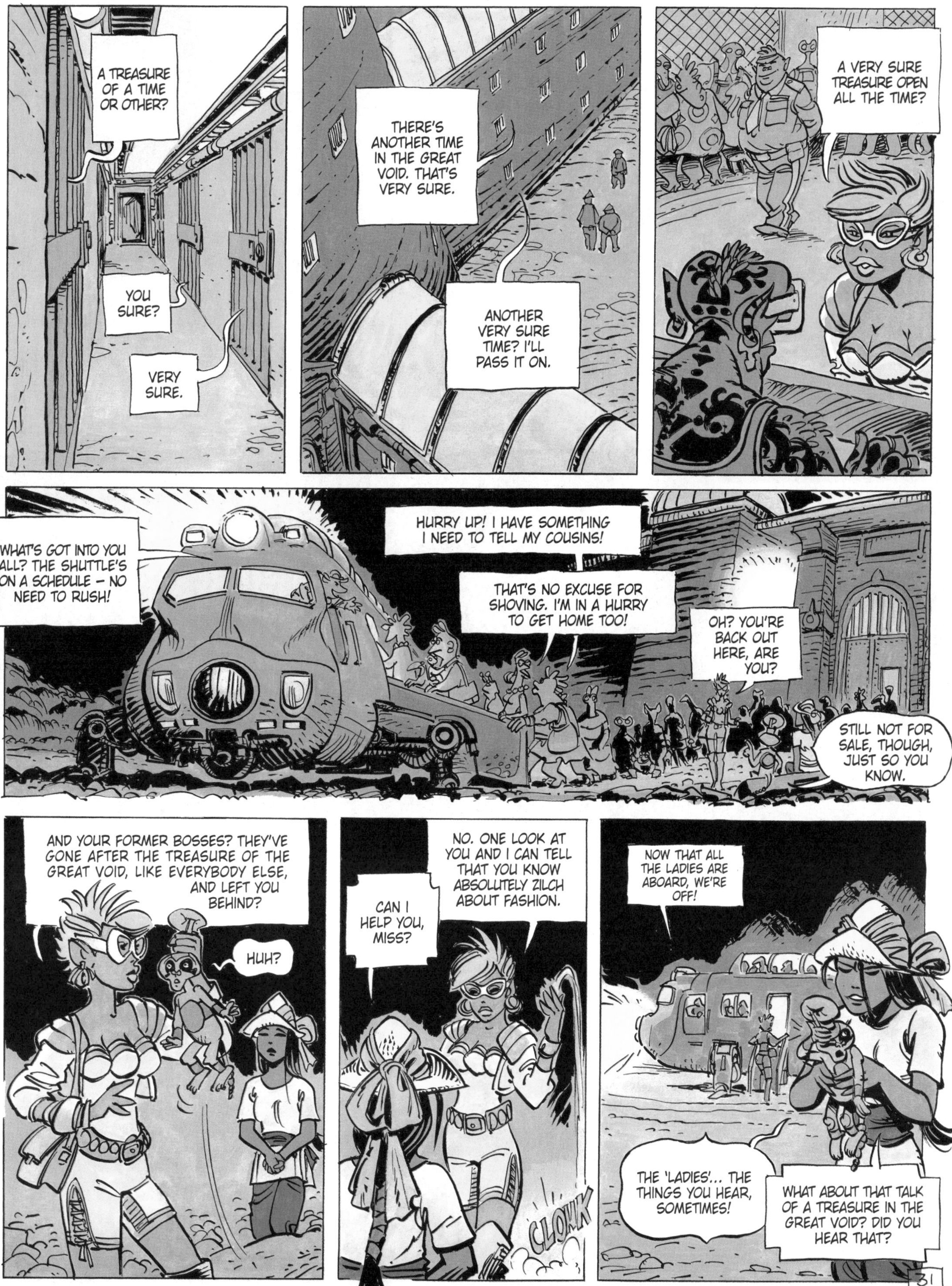
A TREASURE OF A TIME OR OTHER?
YOU SURE?
VERY SURE.
THERE'S ANOTHER TIME IN THE GREAT VOID. THAT'S VERY SURE.
ANOTHER VERY SURE TIME? I'LL PASS IT ON.
A VERY SURE TREASURE OPEN ALL THE TIME?
WHAT'S GOT INTO YOU ALL? THE SHUTTLE'S ON A SCHEDULE – NO NEED TO RUSH!
HURRY UP! I HAVE SOMETHING I NEED TO TELL MY COUSINS!
THAT'S NO EXCUSE FOR SHOVING. I'M IN A HURRY TO GET HOME TOO!
OH? YOU'RE BACK OUT HERE, ARE YOU?
STILL NOT FOR SALE, THOUGH, JUST SO YOU KNOW.
AND YOUR FORMER BOSSES? THEY'VE GONE AFTER THE TREASURE OF THE GREAT VOID, LIKE EVERYBODY ELSE, AND LEFT YOU BEHIND?
HUH?
CAN I HELP YOU, MISS?
NO. ONE LOOK AT YOU AND I CAN TELL THAT YOU KNOW ABSOLUTELY ZILCH ABOUT FASHION.
CLONK
NOW THAT ALL THE LADIES ARE ABOARD, WE'RE OFF!
THE 'LADIES'... THE THINGS YOU HEAR, SOMETIMES!
WHAT ABOUT THAT TALK OF A TREASURE IN THE GREAT VOID? DID YOU HEAR THAT?
31

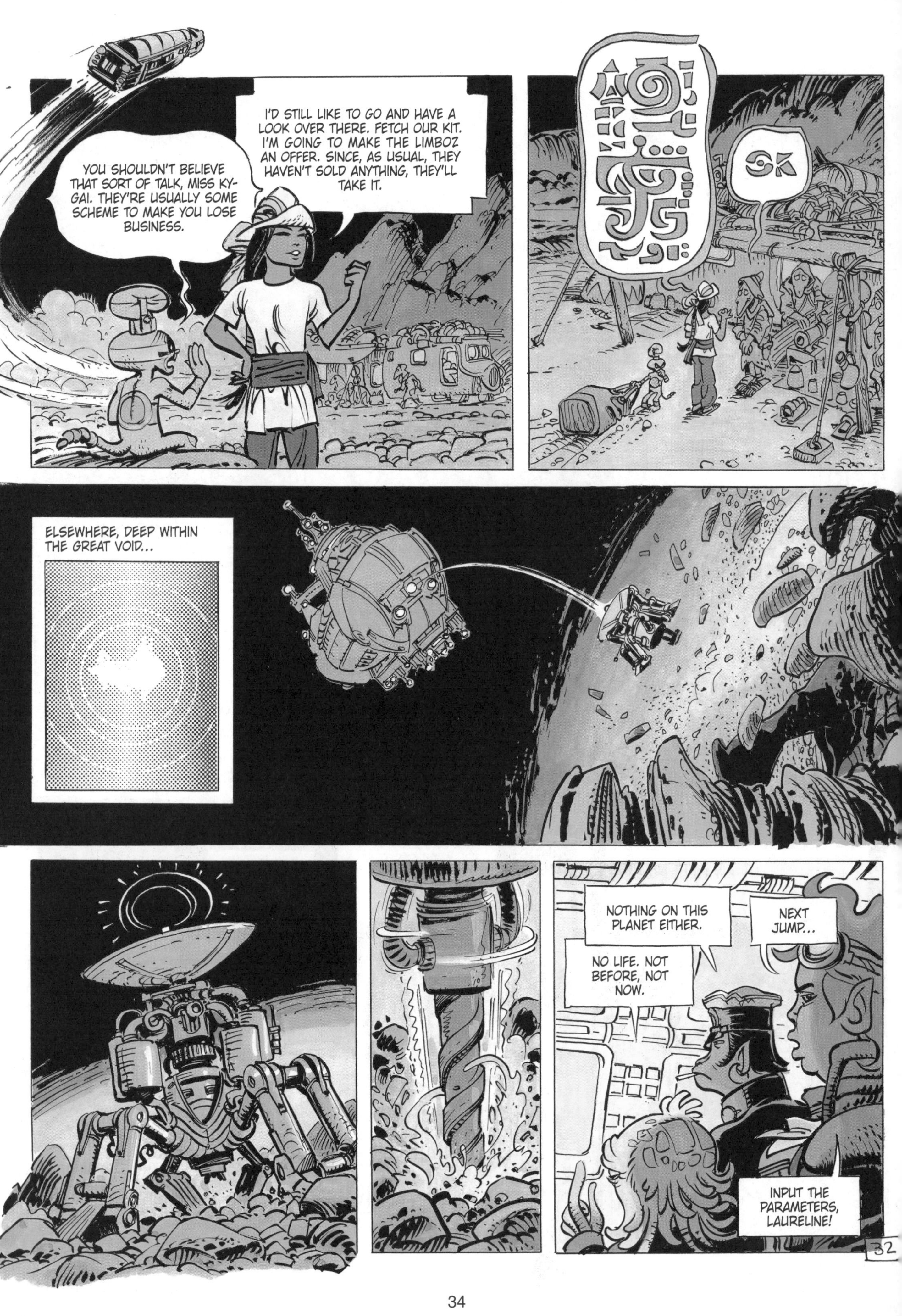

YOU SHOULDN'T BELIEVE THAT SORT OF TALK, MISS KY-GAI. THEY'RE USUALLY SOME SCHEME TO MAKE YOU LOSE BUSINESS.
I'D STILL LIKE TO GO AND HAVE A LOOK OVER THERE. FETCH OUR KIT. I'M GOING TO MAKE THE LIMBOZ AN OFFER. SINCE, AS USUAL, THEY HAVEN'T SOLD ANYTHING, THEY'LL TAKE IT.
ELSEWHERE, DEEP WITHIN THE GREAT VOID...
NOTHING ON THIS PLANET EITHER.
NO LIFE. NOT BEFORE, NOT NOW.
NEXT JUMP...
INPUT THE PARAMETERS, LAURELINE!
32

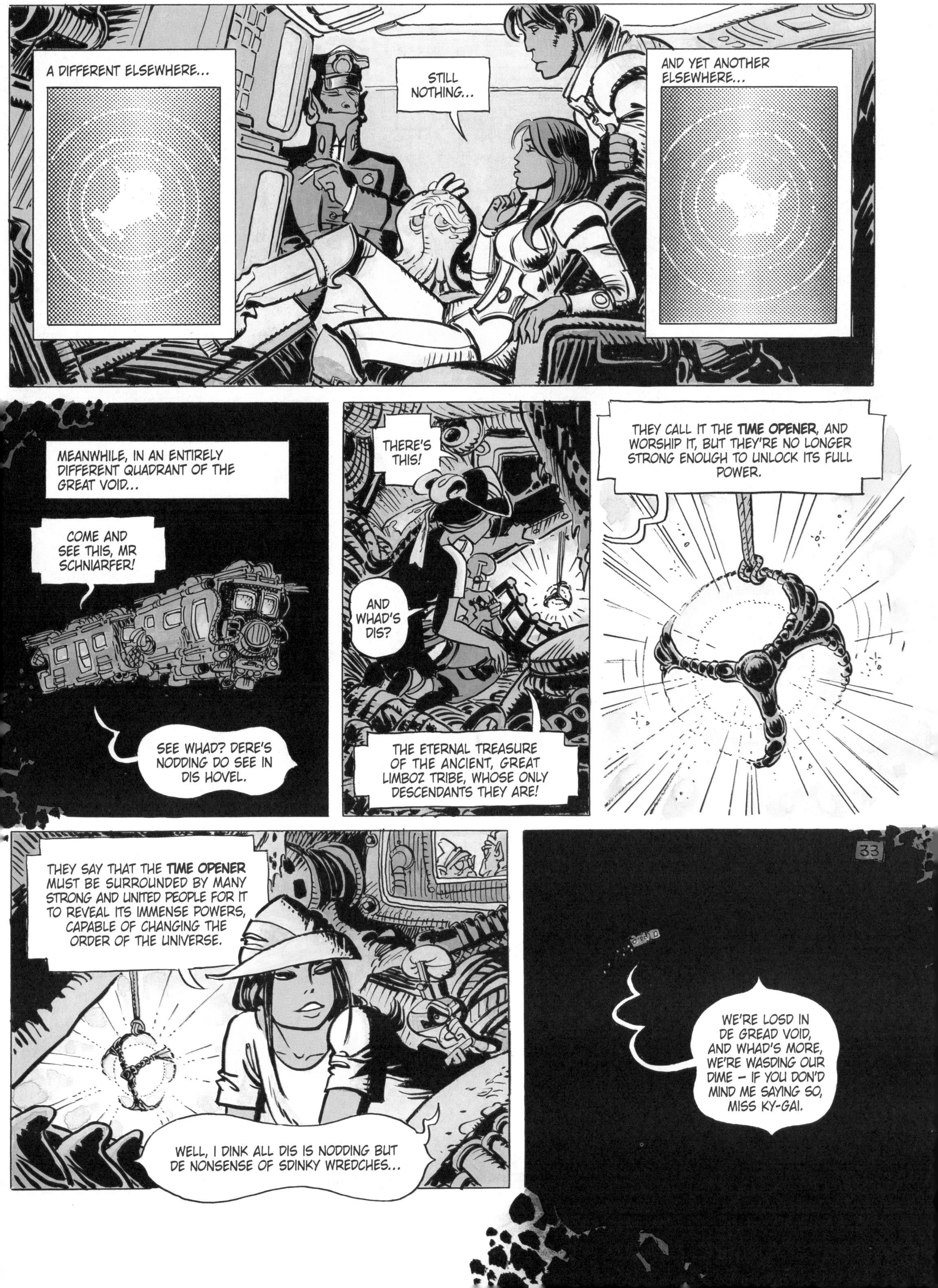
A DIFFERENT ELSEWHERE...
STILL NOTHING...
AND YET ANOTHER ELSEWHERE...
MEANWHILE, IN AN ENTIRELY DIFFERENT QUADRANT OF THE GREAT VOID...
COME AND SEE THIS, MR SCHNIARFER!
SEE WHAD? DERE'S NODDING DO SEE IN DIS HOVEL.
THERE'S THIS!
AND WHAD'S DIS?
THE ETERNAL TREASURE OF THE ANCIENT, GREAT LIMBOZ TRIBE, WHOSE ONLY DESCENDANTS THEY ARE!
THEY CALL IT THE **TIME OPENER**, AND WORSHIP IT, BUT THEY'RE NO LONGER STRONG ENOUGH TO UNLOCK ITS FULL POWER.
THEY SAY THAT THE **TIME OPENER** MUST BE SURROUNDED BY MANY STRONG AND UNITED PEOPLE FOR IT TO REVEAL ITS IMMENSE POWERS, CAPABLE OF CHANGING THE ORDER OF THE UNIVERSE.
WELL, I DINK ALL DIS IS NODDING BUT DE NONSENSE OF SDINKY WREDCHES...
33
WE'RE LOSD IN DE GREAD VOID, AND WHAD'S MORE, WE'RE WASDING OUR DIME – IF YOU DON'D MIND ME SAYING SO, MISS KY-GAI.

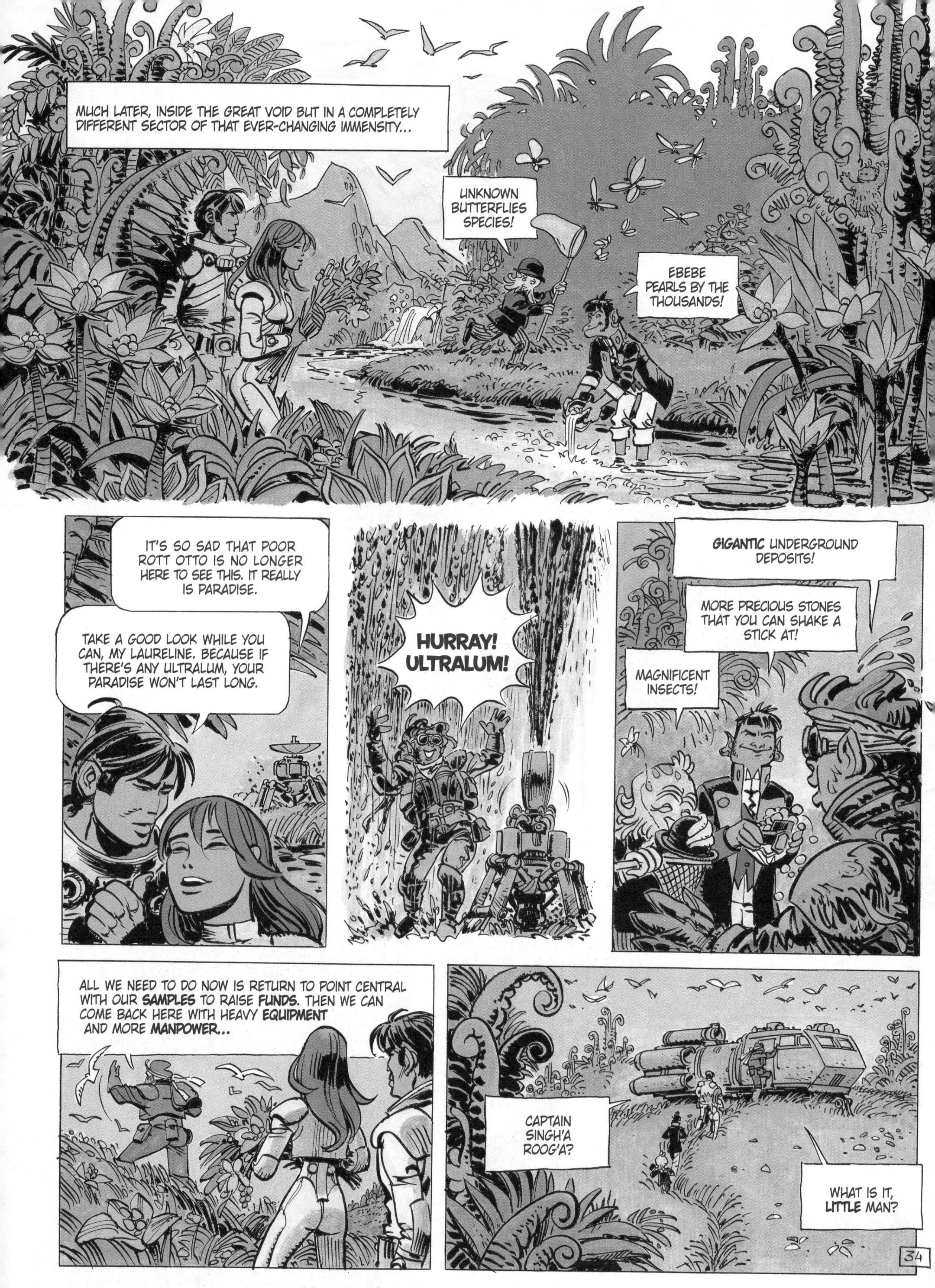

MUCH LATER, INSIDE THE GREAT VOID BUT IN A COMPLETELY DIFFERENT SECTOR OF THAT EVER-CHANGING IMMENSITY...
UNKNOWN BUTTERFLIES SPECIES!
EBEBE PEARLS BY THE THOUSANDS!
IT'S SO SAD THAT POOR ROTT OTTO IS NO LONGER HERE TO SEE THIS. IT REALLY IS PARADISE.
TAKE A GOOD LOOK WHILE YOU CAN, MY LAURELINE. BECAUSE IF THERE'S ANY ULTRALUM, YOUR PARADISE WON'T LAST LONG.
HURRAY! ULTRALUM!
GIGANTIC UNDERGROUND DEPOSITS!
MORE PRECIOUS STONES THAT YOU CAN SHAKE A STICK AT!
MAGNIFICENT INSECTS!
ALL WE NEED TO DO NOW IS RETURN TO POINT CENTRAL WITH OUR SAMPLES TO RAISE FUNDS. THEN WE CAN COME BACK HERE WITH HEAVY EQUIPMENT AND MORE MANPOWER...
CAPTAIN SINGH'A ROOG'A?
WHAT IS IT, LITTLE MAN?
34

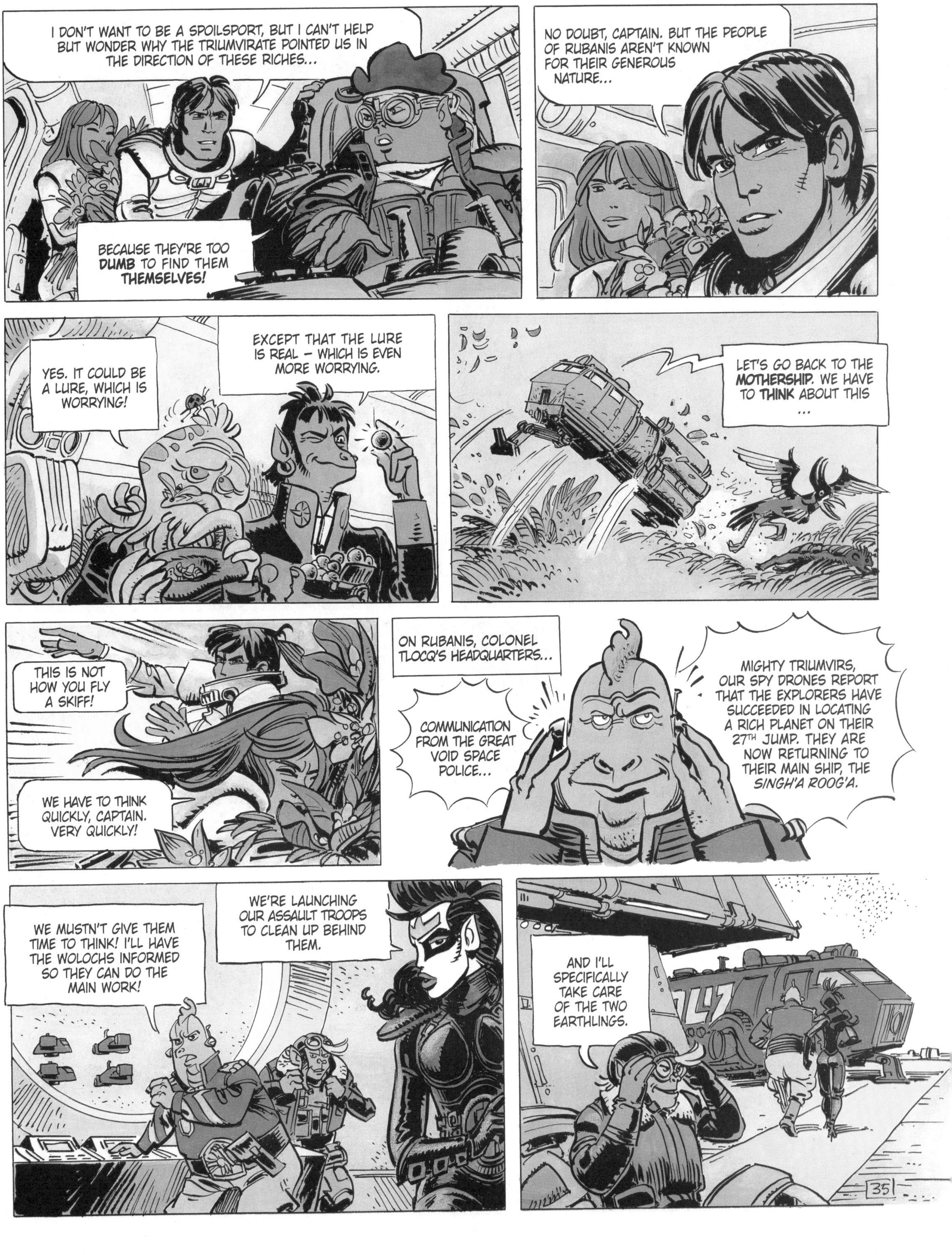
I DON'T WANT TO BE A SPOILSPORT, BUT I CAN'T HELP BUT WONDER WHY THE TRIUMVIRATE POINTED US IN THE DIRECTION OF THESE RICHES...
BECAUSE THEY'RE TOO **DUMB** TO FIND THEM **THEMSELVES!**
NO DOUBT, CAPTAIN. BUT THE PEOPLE OF RUBANIS AREN'T KNOWN FOR THEIR GENEROUS NATURE...
YES. IT COULD BE A LURE, WHICH IS WORRYING!
EXCEPT THAT THE LURE IS REAL – WHICH IS EVEN MORE WORRYING.
LET'S GO BACK TO THE **MOTHERSHIP**. WE HAVE TO **THINK** ABOUT THIS ...
THIS IS NOT HOW YOU FLY A SKIFF!
WE HAVE TO THINK QUICKLY, CAPTAIN. VERY QUICKLY!
ON RUBANIS, COLONEL TLOCQ'S HEADQUARTERS...
COMMUNICATION FROM THE GREAT VOID SPACE POLICE...
MIGHTY TRIUMVIRS, OUR SPY DRONES REPORT THAT THE EXPLORERS HAVE SUCCEEDED IN LOCATING A RICH PLANET ON THEIR 27TH JUMP. THEY ARE NOW RETURNING TO THEIR MAIN SHIP, THE *SINGH'A ROOG'A.*
WE MUSTN'T GIVE THEM TIME TO THINK! I'LL HAVE THE WOLOCHS INFORMED SO THEY CAN DO THE MAIN WORK!
WE'RE LAUNCHING OUR ASSAULT TROOPS TO CLEAN UP BEHIND THEM.
AND I'LL SPECIFICALLY TAKE CARE OF THE TWO EARTHLINGS.
35

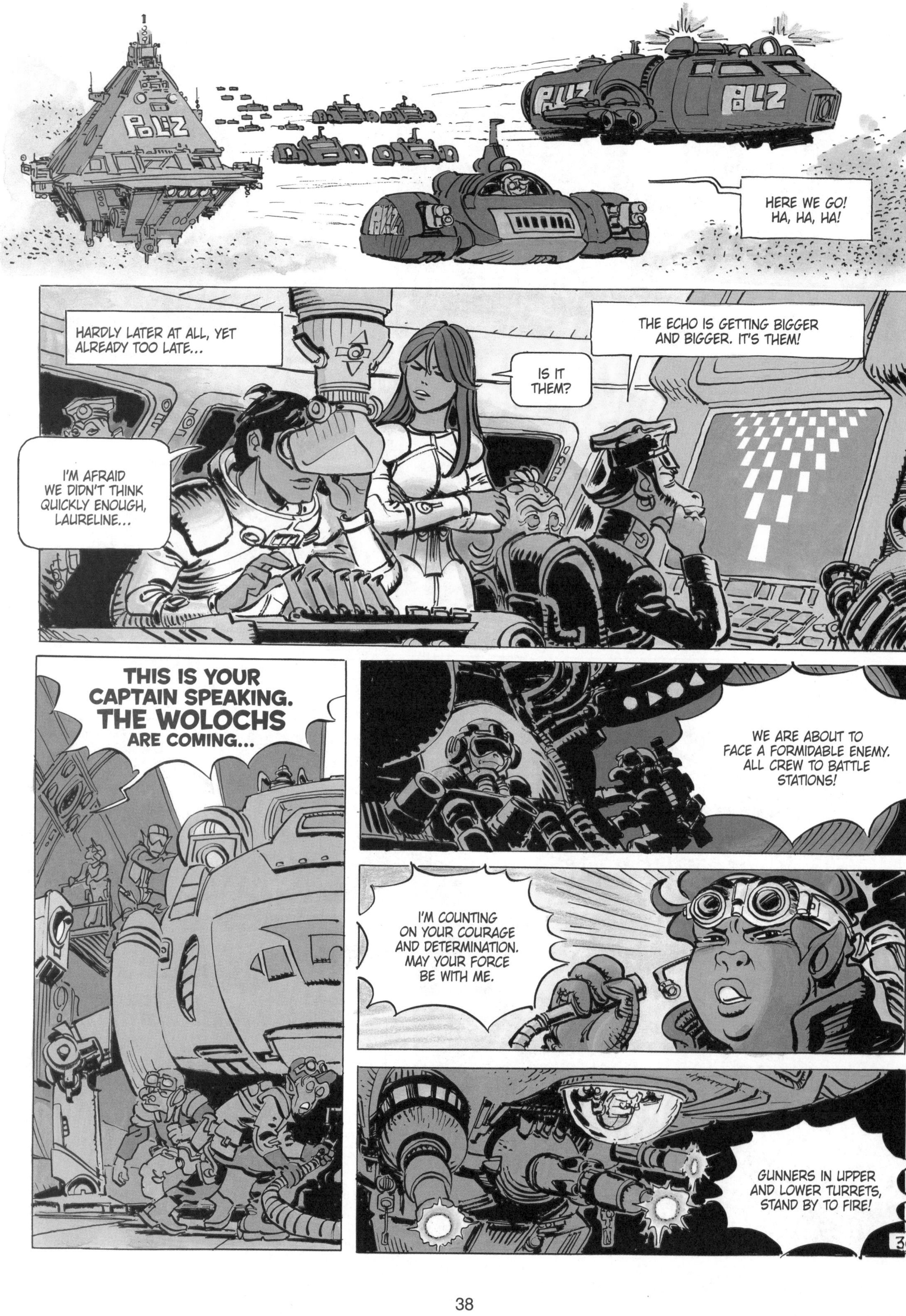
HERE WE GO! HA, HA, HA!
HARDLY LATER AT ALL, YET ALREADY TOO LATE...
IS IT THEM?
THE ECHO IS GETTING BIGGER AND BIGGER. IT'S THEM!
I'M AFRAID WE DIDN'T THINK QUICKLY ENOUGH, LAURELINE...
THIS IS YOUR CAPTAIN SPEAKING. THE WOLOCHS ARE COMING...
WE ARE ABOUT TO FACE A FORMIDABLE ENEMY. ALL CREW TO BATTLE STATIONS!
I'M COUNTING ON YOUR COURAGE AND DETERMINATION. MAY YOUR FORCE BE WITH ME.
GUNNERS IN UPPER AND LOWER TURRETS, STAND BY TO FIRE!
36

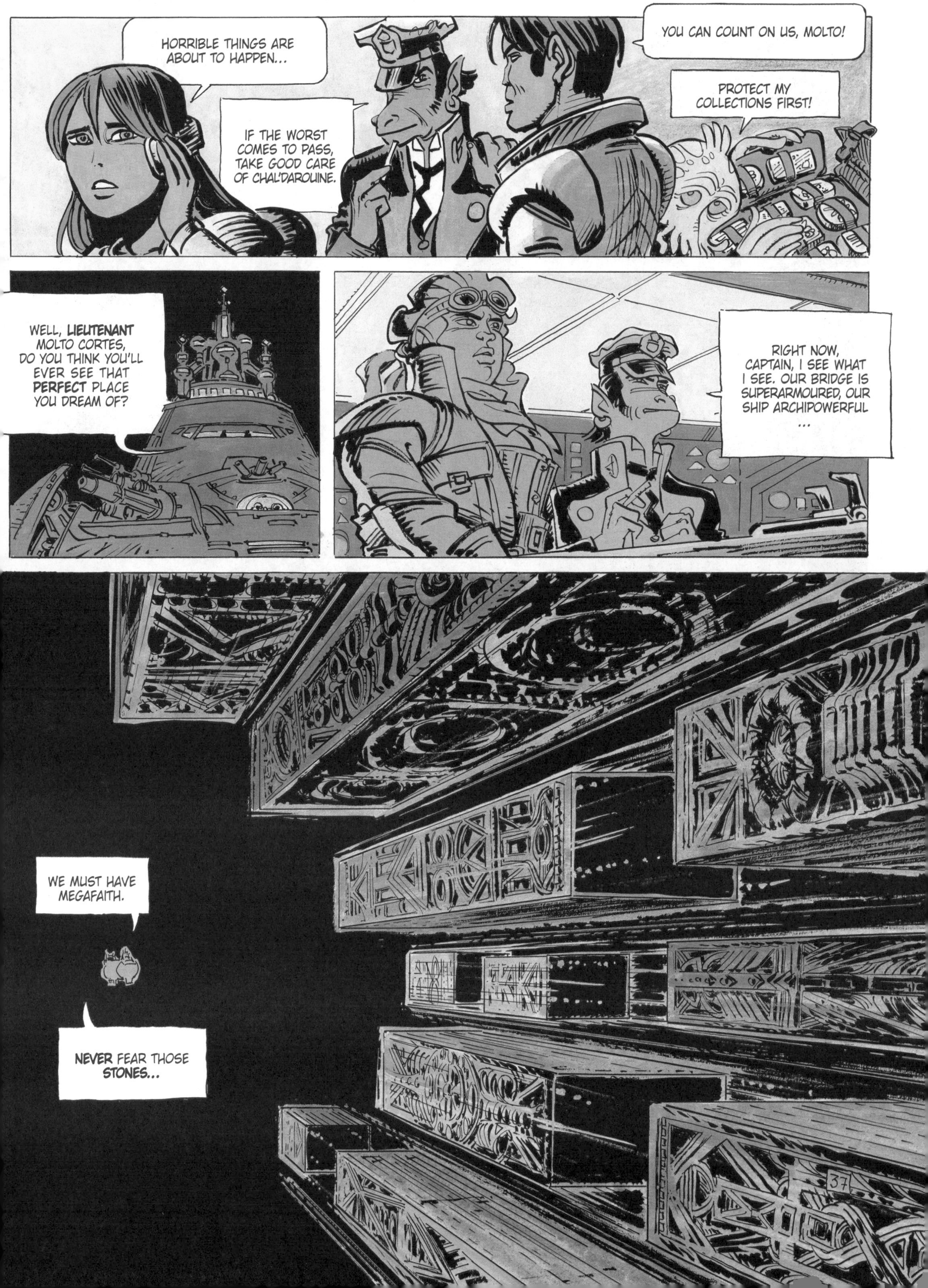
HORRIBLE THINGS ARE ABOUT TO HAPPEN...
IF THE WORST COMES TO PASS, TAKE GOOD CARE OF CHAL'DAROUINE.
YOU CAN COUNT ON US, MOLTO!
PROTECT MY COLLECTIONS FIRST!
WELL, **LIEUTENANT** MOLTO CORTES, DO YOU THINK YOU'LL EVER SEE THAT **PERFECT** PLACE YOU DREAM OF?
RIGHT NOW, CAPTAIN, I SEE WHAT I SEE. OUR BRIDGE IS SUPERARMOURED, OUR SHIP ARCHIPOWERFUL ...
WE MUST HAVE MEGAFAITH.
NEVER FEAR THOSE **STONES...**
37

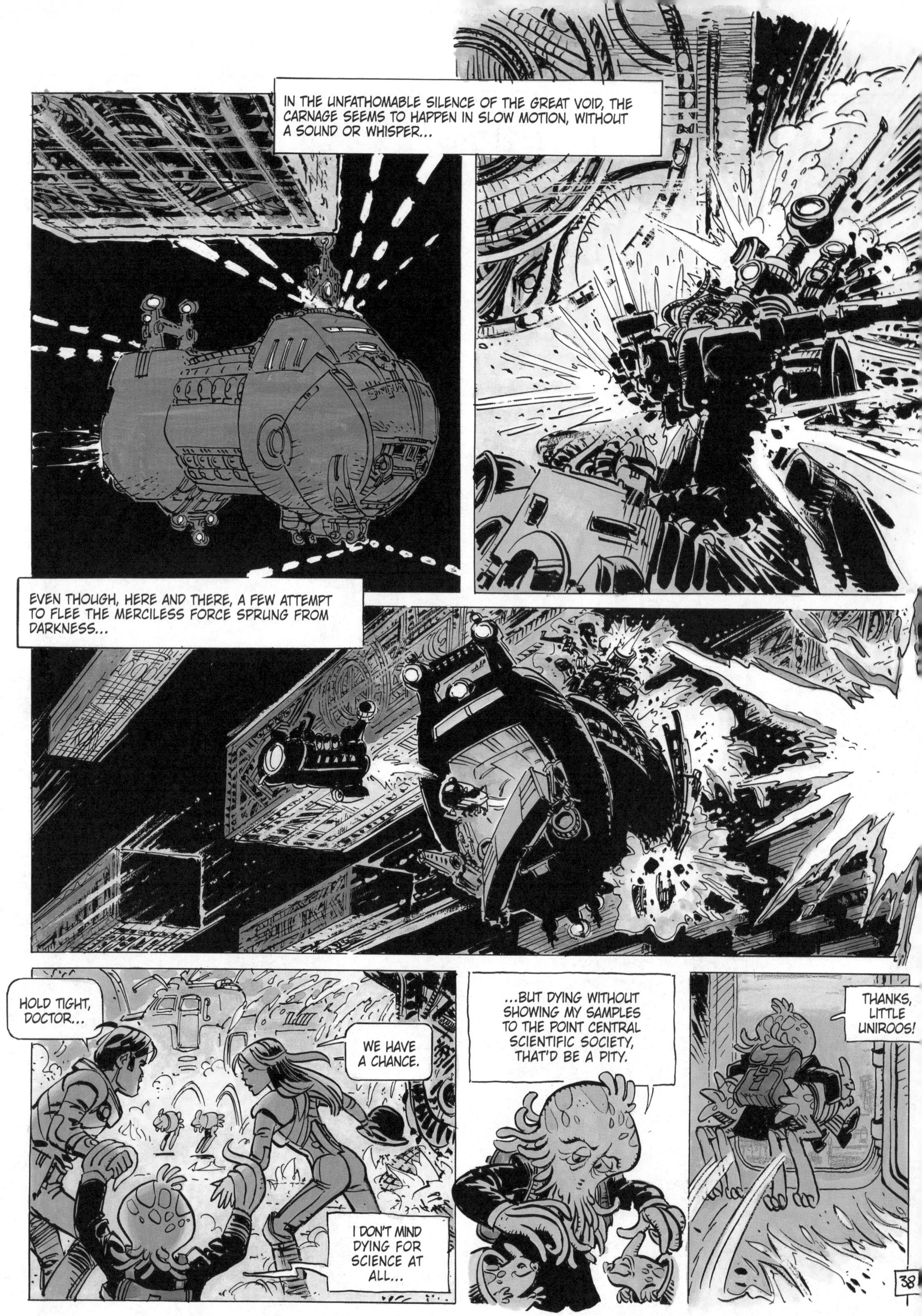
IN THE UNFATHOMABLE SILENCE OF THE GREAT VOID, THE CARNAGE SEEMS TO HAPPEN IN SLOW MOTION, WITHOUT A SOUND OR WHISPER...
EVEN THOUGH, HERE AND THERE, A FEW ATTEMPT TO FLEE THE MERCILESS FORCE SPRUNG FROM DARKNESS...
HOLD TIGHT, DOCTOR...
WE HAVE A CHANCE.
I DON'T MIND DYING FOR SCIENCE AT ALL...
...BUT DYING WITHOUT SHOWING MY SAMPLES TO THE POINT CENTRAL SCIENTIFIC SOCIETY, THAT'D BE A PITY.
THANKS, LITTLE UNIROOS!
38

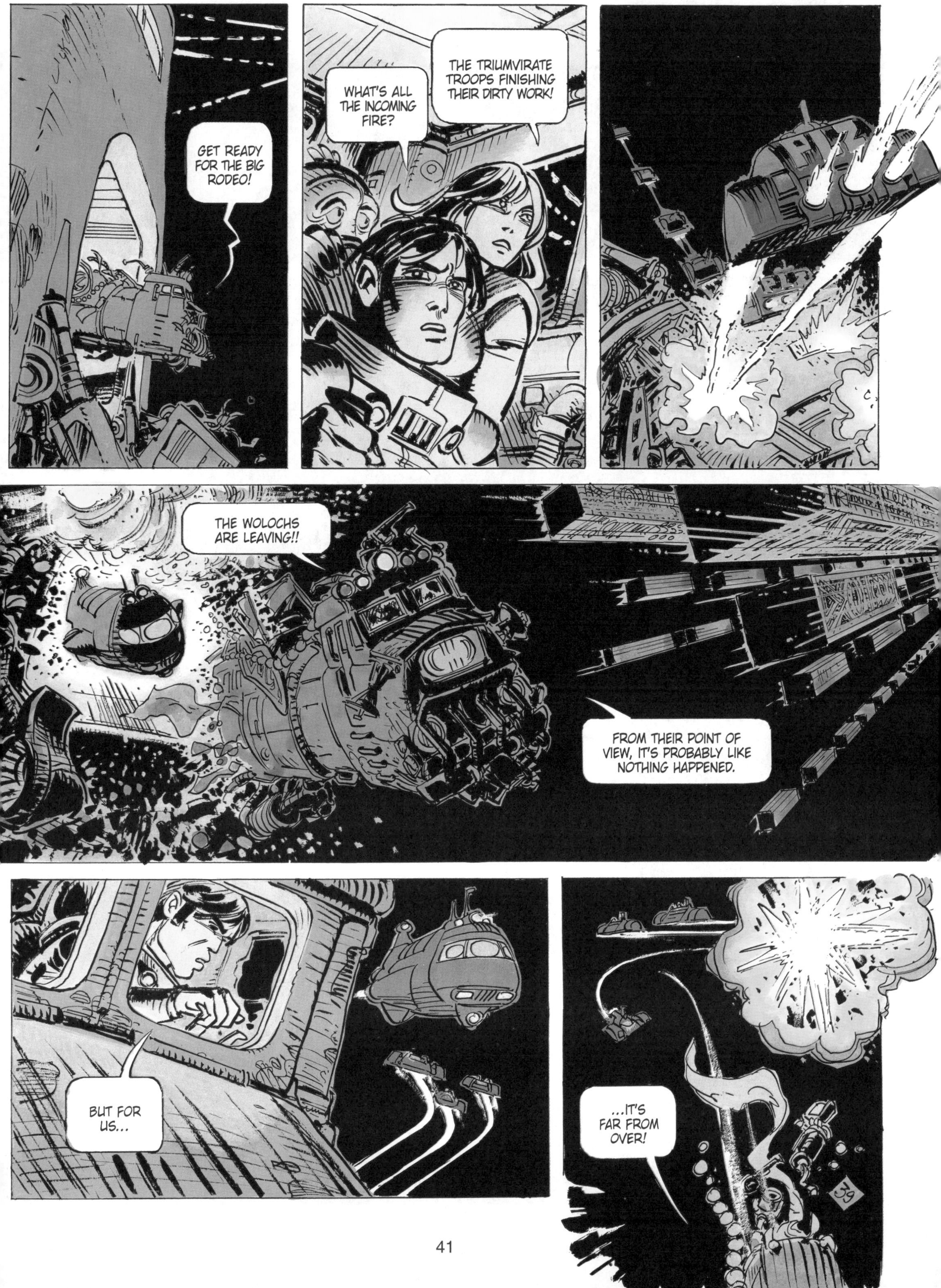
GET READY FOR THE BIG RODEO!
WHAT'S ALL THE INCOMING FIRE?
THE TRIUMVIRATE TROOPS FINISHING THEIR DIRTY WORK!
THE WOLOCHS ARE LEAVING!!
FROM THEIR POINT OF VIEW, IT'S PROBABLY LIKE NOTHING HAPPENED.
BUT FOR US...
...IT'S FAR FROM OVER!
39

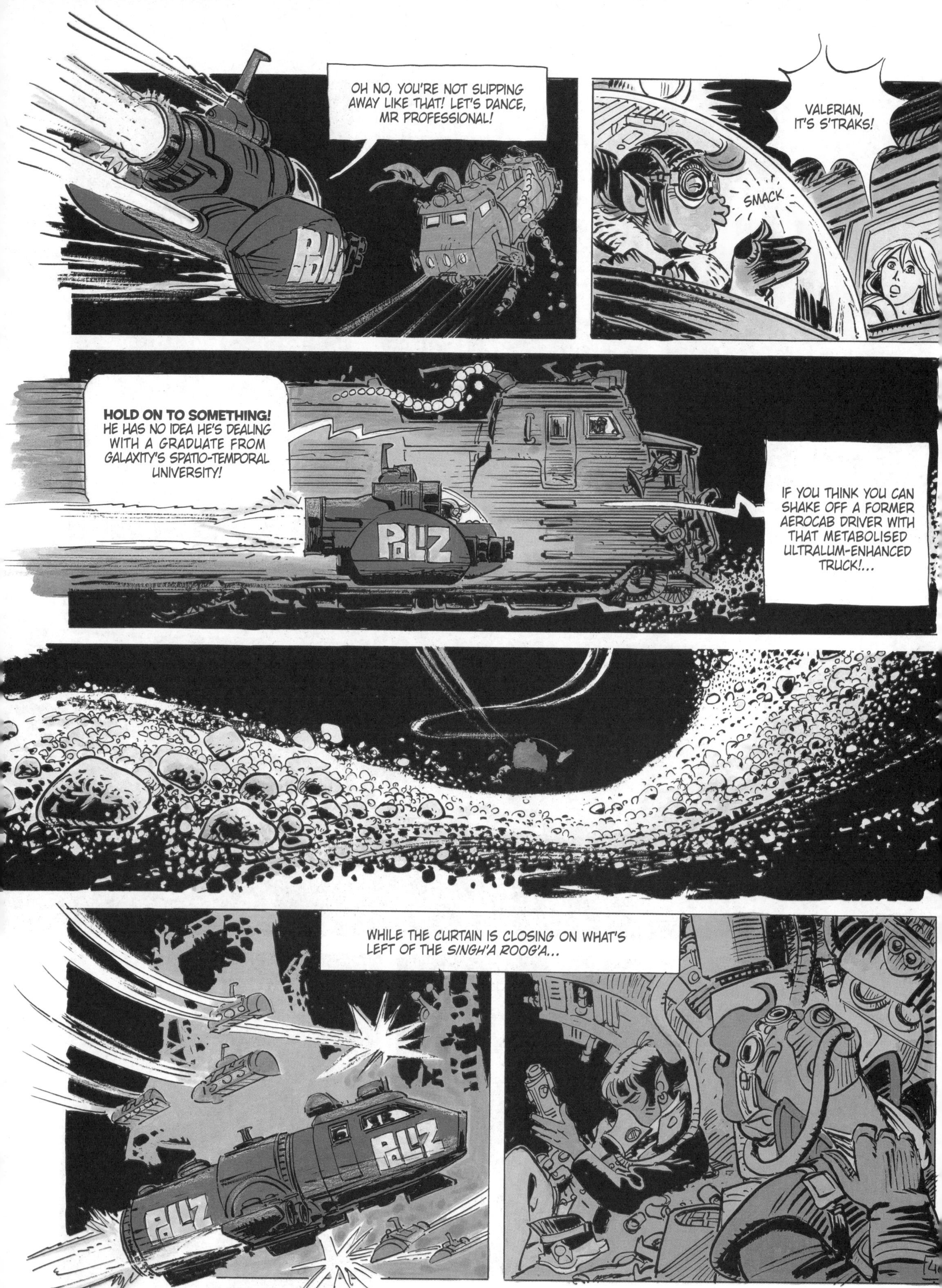
OH NO, YOU'RE NOT SLIPPING AWAY LIKE THAT! LET'S DANCE, MR PROFESSIONAL!
VALERIAN, IT'S S'TRAKS!
SMACK
POLIZ
HOLD ON TO SOMETHING! HE HAS NO IDEA HE'S DEALING WITH A GRADUATE FROM GALAXITY'S SPATIO-TEMPORAL UNIVERSITY!
IF YOU THINK YOU CAN SHAKE OFF A FORMER AEROCAB DRIVER WITH THAT METABOLISED ULTRALUM-ENHANCED TRUCK!...
WHILE THE CURTAIN IS CLOSING ON WHAT'S LEFT OF THE *SINGH'A ROOG'A*...
POLIZ
POLIZ

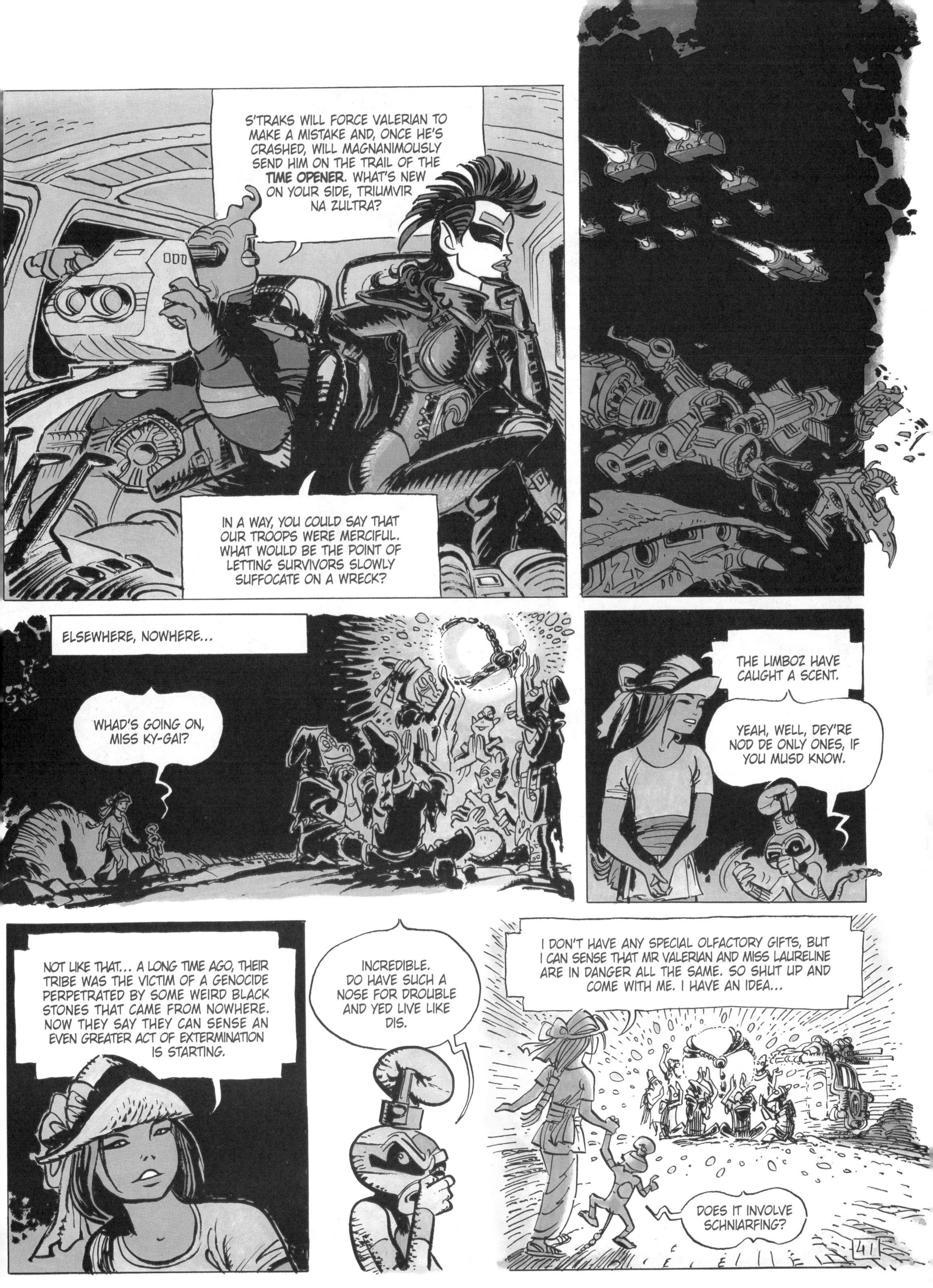
S'TRAKS WILL FORCE VALERIAN TO MAKE A MISTAKE AND, ONCE HE'S CRASHED, WILL MAGNANIMOUSLY SEND HIM ON THE TRAIL OF THE TIME OPENER. WHAT'S NEW ON YOUR SIDE, TRIUMVIR NA ZULTRA?
IN A WAY, YOU COULD SAY THAT OUR TROOPS WERE MERCIFUL. WHAT WOULD BE THE POINT OF LETTING SURVIVORS SLOWLY SUFFOCATE ON A WRECK?
ELSEWHERE, NOWHERE...
WHAD'S GOING ON, MISS KY-GAI?
THE LIMBOZ HAVE CAUGHT A SCENT.
YEAH, WELL, DEY'RE NOD DE ONLY ONES, IF YOU MUSD KNOW.
NOT LIKE THAT... A LONG TIME AGO, THEIR TRIBE WAS THE VICTIM OF A GENOCIDE PERPETRATED BY SOME WEIRD BLACK STONES THAT CAME FROM NOWHERE. NOW THEY SAY THEY CAN SENSE AN EVEN GREATER ACT OF EXTERMINATION IS STARTING.
INCREDIBLE. DO HAVE SUCH A NOSE FOR DROUBLE AND YED LIVE LIKE DIS.
I DON'T HAVE ANY SPECIAL OLFACTORY GIFTS, BUT I CAN SENSE THAT MR VALERIAN AND MISS LAURELINE ARE IN DANGER ALL THE SAME. SO SHUT UP AND COME WITH ME. I HAVE AN IDEA...
DOES IT INVOLVE SCHNIARFING?
41

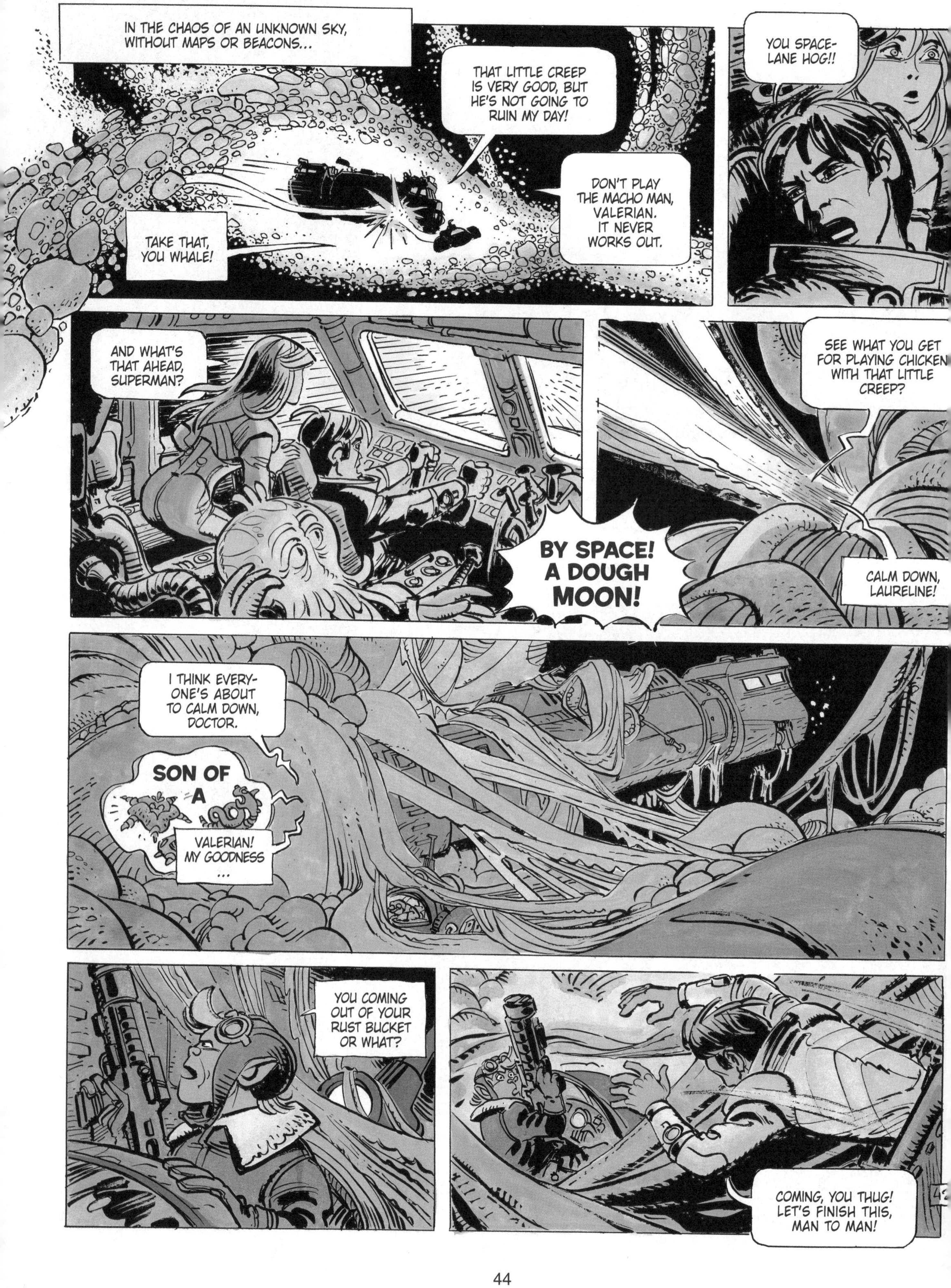
IN THE CHAOS OF AN UNKNOWN SKY, WITHOUT MAPS OR BEACONS...
THAT LITTLE CREEP IS VERY GOOD, BUT HE'S NOT GOING TO RUIN MY DAY!
TAKE THAT, YOU WHALE!
DON'T PLAY THE MACHO MAN, VALERIAN. IT NEVER WORKS OUT.
YOU SPACE-LANE HOG!!
AND WHAT'S THAT AHEAD, SUPERMAN?
BY SPACE! A DOUGH MOON!
SEE WHAT YOU GET FOR PLAYING CHICKEN WITH THAT LITTLE CREEP?
CALM DOWN, LAURELINE!
I THINK EVERY-ONE'S ABOUT TO CALM DOWN, DOCTOR.
SON OF A
VALERIAN! MY GOODNESS ...
YOU COMING OUT OF YOUR RUST BUCKET OR WHAT?
COMING, YOU THUG! LET'S FINISH THIS, MAN TO MAN!

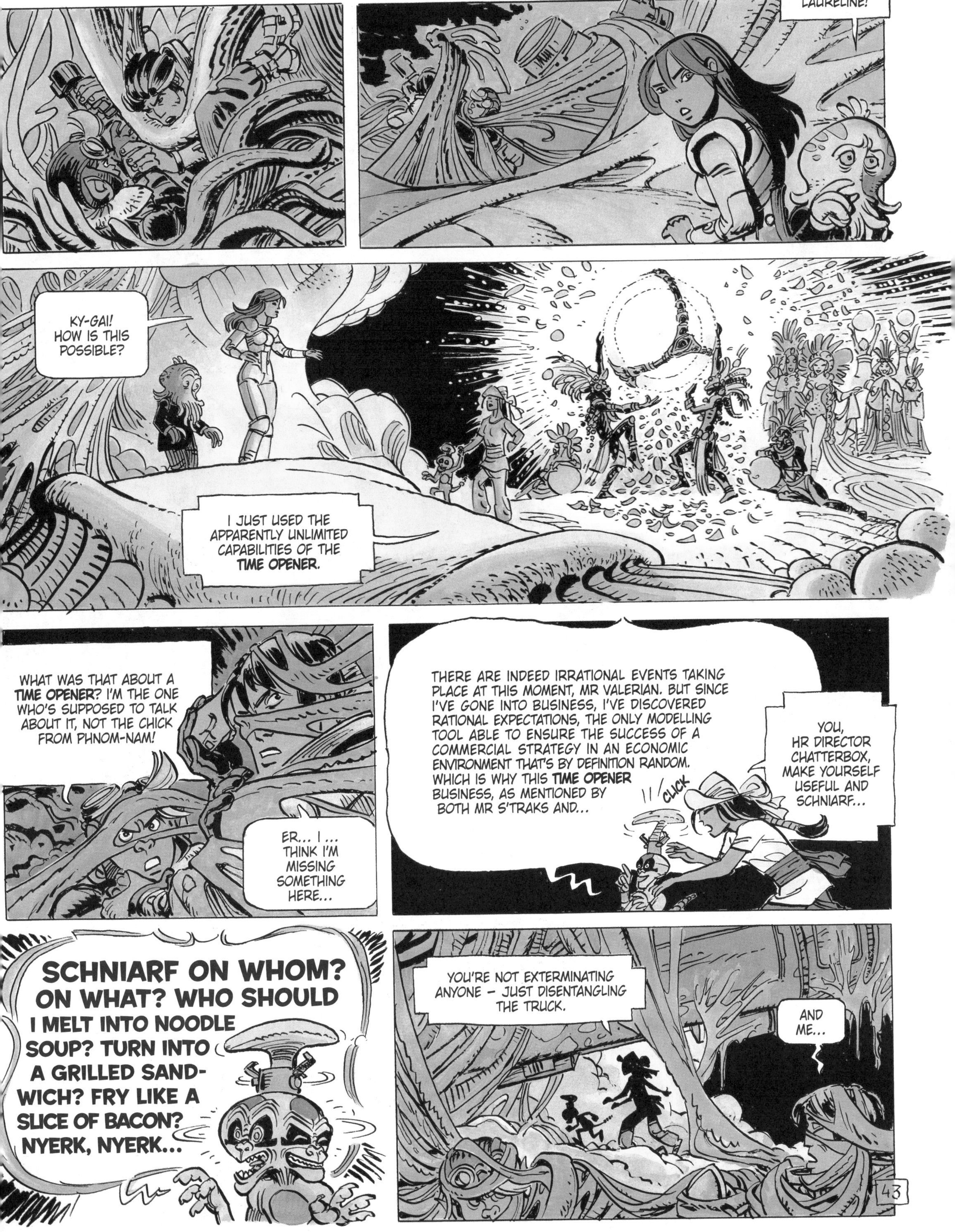
LAURELINE!
KY-GAI! HOW IS THIS POSSIBLE?
I JUST USED THE APPARENTLY UNLIMITED CAPABILITIES OF THE TIME OPENER.
WHAT WAS THAT ABOUT A TIME OPENER? I'M THE ONE WHO'S SUPPOSED TO TALK ABOUT IT, NOT THE CHICK FROM PHNOM-NAM!
ER... I ... THINK I'M MISSING SOMETHING HERE...
THERE ARE INDEED IRRATIONAL EVENTS TAKING PLACE AT THIS MOMENT, MR VALERIAN. BUT SINCE I'VE GONE INTO BUSINESS, I'VE DISCOVERED RATIONAL EXPECTATIONS, THE ONLY MODELLING TOOL ABLE TO ENSURE THE SUCCESS OF A COMMERCIAL STRATEGY IN AN ECONOMIC ENVIRONMENT THAT'S BY DEFINITION RANDOM. WHICH IS WHY THIS TIME OPENER BUSINESS, AS MENTIONED BY BOTH MR S'TRAKS AND...
CLICK
YOU, HR DIRECTOR CHATTERBOX, MAKE YOURSELF USEFUL AND SCHNIARF...
SCHNIARF ON WHOM? ON WHAT? WHO SHOULD I MELT INTO NOODLE SOUP? TURN INTO A GRILLED SANDWICH? FRY LIKE A SLICE OF BACON? NYERK, NYERK...
YOU'RE NOT EXTERMINATING ANYONE – JUST DISENTANGLING THE TRUCK.
AND ME...
43

THIS IS THE **TIME OPENER**?

YES, MISS LAURELINE. IF YOU WANT SOMETHING REALLY HARD, THE **TIME OPENER** CAN GIVE IT TO YOU. WOULD YOU LIKE TO TRY?

WELL... I'M NOT SURE... YES... I BELIEVE...

THE LIMBOZ TOLD ME THAT BELIEVING IS SEEING.

THEN I WANT TO SEE MY PLANET, **EARTH**!

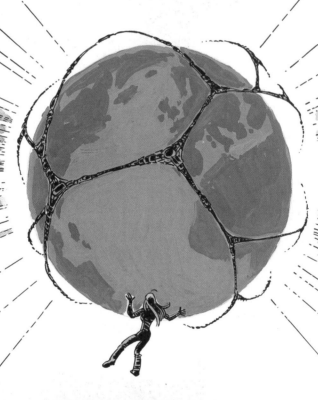

IF I SAW WHAT I THINK I SAW, IT'S A MIRACLE OF SCIENCE!

ARE YOU ALL RIGHT, MISS LAURELINE?

JUST A LITTLE SHAKEN.

IT'S OVER. WE'RE NOT STRONG ENOUGH TO GO ANY FURTHER.

NOT STRONG ENOUGH ... THIS TIME.

HELLO?

46

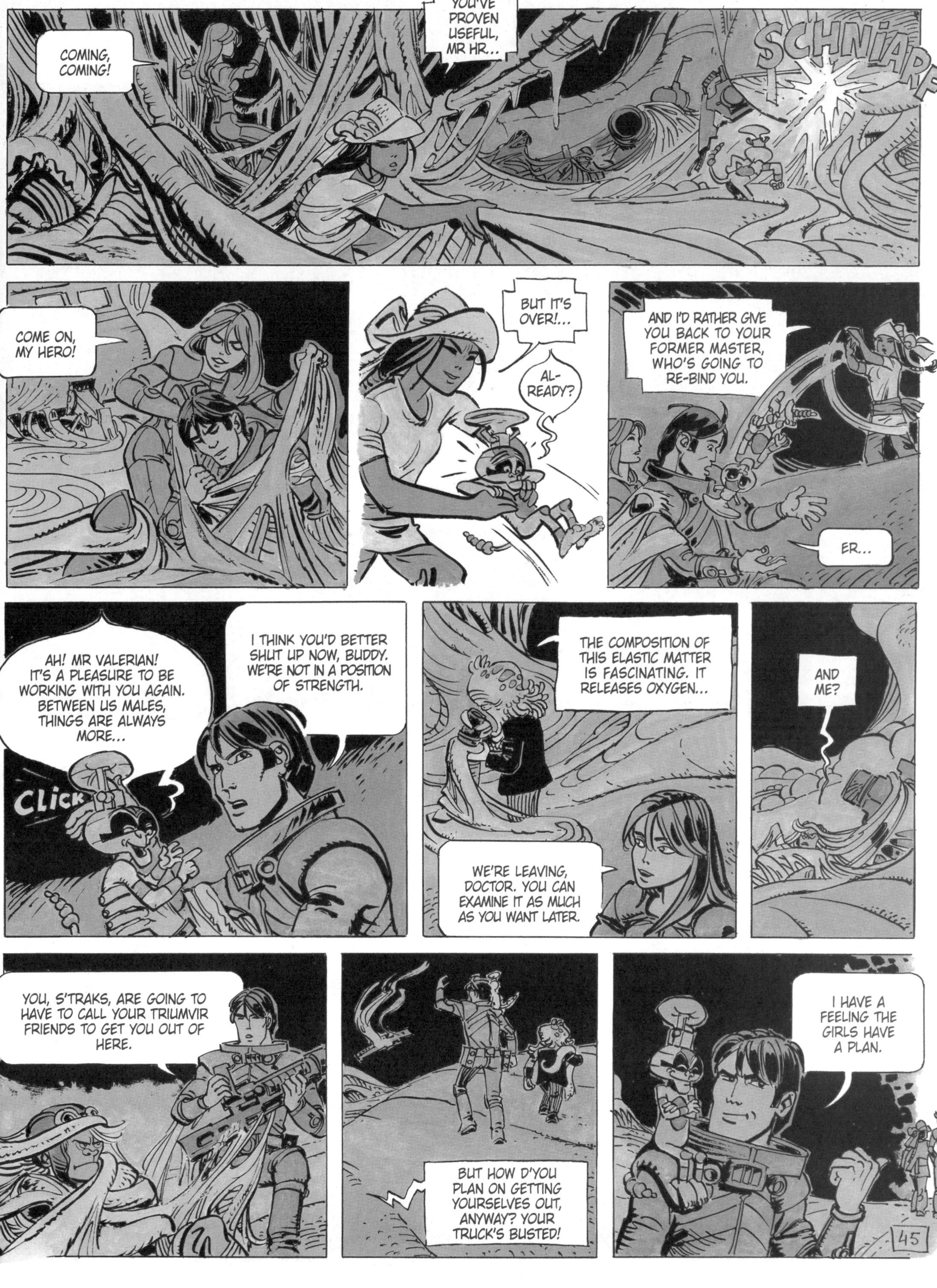
COMING, COMING!
YOU'VE PROVEN USEFUL, MR HR...
SCHNIARF
COME ON, MY HERO!
BUT IT'S OVER!...
AL-READY?
AND I'D RATHER GIVE YOU BACK TO YOUR FORMER MASTER, WHO'S GOING TO RE-BIND YOU.
ER...
AH! MR VALERIAN! IT'S A PLEASURE TO BE WORKING WITH YOU AGAIN. BETWEEN US MALES, THINGS ARE ALWAYS MORE...
CLICK
I THINK YOU'D BETTER SHUT UP NOW, BUDDY. WE'RE NOT IN A POSITION OF STRENGTH.
THE COMPOSITION OF THIS ELASTIC MATTER IS FASCINATING. IT RELEASES OXYGEN...
WE'RE LEAVING, DOCTOR. YOU CAN EXAMINE IT AS MUCH AS YOU WANT LATER.
AND ME?
YOU, S'TRAKS, ARE GOING TO HAVE TO CALL YOUR TRIUMVIR FRIENDS TO GET YOU OUT OF HERE.
BUT HOW D'YOU PLAN ON GETTING YOURSELVES OUT, ANYWAY? YOUR TRUCK'S BUSTED!
I HAVE A FEELING THE GIRLS HAVE A PLAN.
45

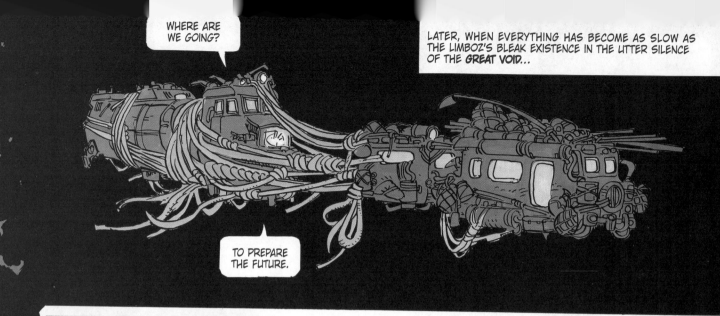

WHERE ARE WE GOING?

LATER, WHEN EVERYTHING HAS BECOME AS SLOW AS THE LIMBOZ'S BLEAK EXISTENCE IN THE UTTER SILENCE OF THE **GREAT VOID**...

TO PREPARE THE FUTURE.

I SAW **EARTH**, VALERIAN. AND IF I SAW IT, IT MEANS IT'S SOMEWHERE NOT SO DISTANT.

MISS LAURELINE, **THE TSHUNG!**

IT CAME BACK WITH THE ANSWER. YOUR FRIENDS ARE WAITING FOR US.

CHEEP

WHO? WHERE? IF YOU DON'T MIND ME ASKING?...

YOU'LL SEE, BOYS. YOU'LL SEE...

PFFFFF...

ANNOYING, ISN'T IT, BOSS?

46

P. CHRISTIN
AND
JC MEZIERES
2006_

NEXT VOLUME **THE TIME OPENER**

END
OF THE
EPISODE